Love Redeemed

LAUREL RIDGE SERIES, BOOK #4

TARA BAISDEN

STERLING RIDGE PRESS LLC

Cover designed by Sterling Ridge Press LLC

Published by: Sterling Ridge Press, LLC www.sterlingridgepress.com

ISBN: 978-1-966093-06-0
Printed in the United States of America

First Edition: November 2024

For permissions, contact: tara@tarabaisden.com or visit www.tarabaisden.com

Contents

About The Author

Tara Baisden is a Contemporary Inspirational Romance author who proudly calls the beautiful state of West Virginia her home. Nestled on a sprawling mountainous property, she is surrounded by the peace and serenity of nature. Her days are happily spent in the quiet of country life, writing heartwarming stories of love, faith, and second chances. Tara also enjoys quilting, working in her garden, tending to her beloved pets, and soaking in the beauty of her surroundings.

With deep roots in West Virginia, family is everything to Tara. One of her favorite pastimes is gathering on the front porch with loved ones, sharing stories, laughter, and enjoying the simple, meaningful moments that life offers. When she's not crafting her novels, Tara can often be found exploring the rich history of her home state, visiting local historical sites, and, of course, stopping by every bookstore she passes! Her passion for reading and discovery always fuels her next adventure.

Tara is the author of the Laurel Ridges Series of novels, which includes: Season of Hope, Finding Grace, His Perfect Plan, Love Redeemed, Snowbound Blessings, and Sheltered Hearts all of which have been beloved by fans of inspirational romance. Her novels reflect her love for faith, family, and the timeless beauty of West Virginia.

Known for her sweet and clean romances, she creates characters that feel like family and settings that make readers want to visit again and again.

You can find out more about Tara and her latest releases at www.tarabaisden.com or follow her on social media for updates and behind-the-scenes glimpses of her writing process. Stay connected—you won't want to miss the heartfelt stories of love and family she has in store!

Also by Tara Baisden

Dedication

To all those who have faced loss and found the strength to heal—this one's for you. May you always find hope in new beginnings, comfort in the warmth of love, and peace in the belief that even the deepest scars can heal.

And to those who believe in the magic of Christmas, thank you for keeping the wonder alive. May your holiday season be filled with joy, light, and just a little bit of Christmas magic.

About Laurel Ridge

Welcome to the fictional town of Laurel Ridge, West Virginia!

Nestled deep in the heart of the Appalachian Mountains, Laurel Ridge is a place where time slows down, allowing visitors and residents alike to enjoy life's simple pleasures. With its quaint, brick-paved streets, historic storefronts, and the ever-present backdrop of rolling hills and dense forests, Laurel Ridge is a hidden gem that attracts tourists looking for both serenity and adventure.

A Rich History

The town was founded in the early 1800s by pioneering settlers who were drawn to the fertile land and abundant natural resources of the region. Laurel Ridge began as a small logging community, relying on the towering forests that covered the surrounding mountains. The New River, one of the oldest rivers in the world, provided an essential transportation route for lumber, as well as a lifeline for the early settlers.

As the years passed, the town evolved from a logging outpost into a thriving hub for craftspeople and artisans. By the late 19th century, it had developed a reputation for its hand-crafted furniture, textiles, and pottery, all made by skilled locals. The town's proximity to the New River also made it a destination for adventurous souls seeking to kayak, fish, or hike along the riverbanks.

A Place of Renewal

Though the logging industry faded by the early 20th century, Laurel Ridge adapted to the changing times. Its natural beauty and deep connection to West Virginia's mountain heritage drew travelers from near and far, transforming it into a beloved tourist destination. Local shops, run by generations of the same families, line the town square, offering handmade goods, locally sourced foods, and, most of all, warm hospitality.

The town's signature event, the Harvest Festival, began in the 1930s, celebrating the craftsmanship, music, and traditions passed down through the generations. Each year, visitors flock to enjoy live Ap-

palachian music, taste locally grown produce, and witness demonstra-
tions of old-world techniques like blacksmithing and weaving.

A Town of Faith and Community

At the heart of the town stands Laurel Ridge Community Church, a
small, white clapboard building with a steeple that reaches toward the
sky. Built in 1876, the church has been a pillar of faith and strength
for the community for over a century. Its bell, crafted by the town's
original blacksmith, has been ringing on Sunday mornings ever since,
calling townsfolk to worship and reminding everyone of the enduring
values of faith, hope, and love.
The church's history is intertwined with the town's, serving as a refuge
in difficult times and a gathering place in moments of joy. Over the
years, the church has grown to include an outreach center that sup-
ports local families and tourists in need, providing everything from
free meals to spiritual counseling. The church's welcoming atmosphere reflects the town's deep sense of unity and service.

A Growing Tourist Haven

Today, Laurel Ridge has grown to a population of around five thousand people, yet it has managed to retain its small-town charm. Its
thriving tourist industry draws visitors year-round. Tourists can stroll
through mom-and-pop shops, and dine at the beloved Martha's Diner, famous for its homemade pies and retro charm. The town square,
with its white gazebo surrounded by flowering bushes, is often the site

of outdoor concerts and farmers' markets, creating a sense of nostalgia and small-town pride.

For nature lovers, the New River offers breathtaking views and the thrill of adventure, whether it's fishing in its crystal blue waters or hiking along the rugged trails that weave through the wilderness. Tourists and locals alike cherish the scenic beauty, often finding peace in the simple pleasures of watching the river flow or taking in the panoramic vistas of the Appalachian Mountains.

Laurel Ridge, with its rich history, strong community spirit, and natural beauty, is more than just a tourist destination—it's a place where past and present blend seamlessly, offering everyone who visits a chance to experience the best of West Virginia's mountain heritage.

You'll find that Laurel Ridge is a town that captures the heart.

Welcome to Laurel Ridge. I hope you fall in love with this charming small town and its residents.

Chapter 1

Snow drifted down like whispered prayers over Laurel Ridge, each flake catching the glow of Christmas lights strung across Main Street. Emma Whitman's hands tightened around the steering wheel of her SUV, the soft leather cool beneath her trembling fingers. The familiar streets stretched before her like pages from an old storybook—one she'd read a thousand times, but somehow felt different now.

Through the windshield, the town unfurled like a living Christmas card. Twinkling lights draped storefront windows in crisp halos of color, while fresh evergreen wreaths adorned century-old doors, their red ribbons dancing in the evening breeze. The brick-paved streets, dusted with snow, echoed with the gentle crunch of her tires.

Martha's Diner glowed like a beacon ahead, its neon coffee cup sign flickering against the twilight sky. Through frosted windows, she caught glimpses of families gathered around steaming mugs of hot cocoa. The sight tugged at something deep within her—memories of countless mornings spent in those worn vinyl booths with Wendy and Leah, her childhood best friends, dreaming up their futures over endless stacks of blueberry pancakes.

But those days felt like they belonged to someone else now, buried beneath the weight of everything she'd lost and everything that had changed.

Emma absently touched the scar on her neck, a habit she'd developed since the accident. After the long drive from Pittsburgh with a small rental trailer in tow, she'd finally arrived. The trailer carried only the essentials she'd kept after selling nearly everything else—her townhouse, her furniture, the life she'd built over seventeen years reduced to whatever would fit in a six-foot trailer.

"You're here," she reminded herself, exhaling slowly as her breath fogged the window. "You made it."

Yet even as the familiar sights of home surrounded her, that hollow ache persisted in her chest. No amount of twinkling lights or holiday cheer could fully mask the grief and uncertainty that had driven her back to Laurel Ridge. Nor could they chase away the haunting sense of being lost on a dead-end road, wondering if she'd ever find her way forward in life again.

Moving back to Laurel Ridge had been her choice—a desperate grab at healing, at finding solid ground to start over again. But as she navigated the snow-covered streets, doubt crept in like the evening chill. Could this place really offer the solace she yearned for? Or would it simply serve as another reminder of everything that had changed?

As Emma turned onto the narrow lane leading to the parsonage, the church where Andrew pastored came into view. Its white steeple rose against the darkening sky. Warm light spilled from arched windows like liquid gold. Laurel Ridge Community Church had been the backdrop for countless moments in her life—birthday parties that echoed through the recreation hall, potluck dinners that filled the air with the scent of casseroles and fellowship, Christmas Eve services where candles flickered like earthbound stars.

The driveway to Andrew's home wound between towering evergreens, their snow-laden branches bowing low as if in greeting. The parsonage itself stood warm and welcoming, its mid-century charm enhanced by garlands and white lights that turned the falling snow into dancing diamonds. Emma parked beside Andrew's silver pickup, killed the engine, and sat in the sudden silence, her heart drumming an unsteady rhythm against her ribs.

The front door swung open before she could gather her courage.

"Well, if it isn't the prodigal sister returning!" Andrew's voice carried across the snow-covered yard as she stepped out into the crisp evening air.

Despite herself, Emma's lips curved into a tired smile. "I didn't know you'd be keeping watch like a hawk," she called back.

"Please. I've only been pacing by the window for the last hour." Andrew's eyes sparkled with familiar mischief as he crunched through the snow toward her. "I might have worn a path on my rug."

"It's good to see you, bub," Emma said, letting herself be enveloped in his bear hug.

"You've been missed, Em," he murmured, his embrace carrying all the protective affection only a big brother could muster.

"Well, I'm back now," she said.

"Let's get you inside before you turn into an icicle. Though that might make the Sunday sermon more interesting—'The Miraculous Frozen Sister.'"

Emma rolled her eyes, but the knot in her chest loosened slightly. "Help me grab a few things? I packed an overnight bag and a small suitcase, so I wouldn't have to dig through the trailer until tomorrow."

They retrieved her suitcase and essentials from the SUV, then climbed the porch steps, snow crunching beneath their boots. The moment Emma stepped inside, warmth wrapped around her like a familiar blanket. Fresh evergreen scented the air from the Christmas tree nestled by the stone fireplace. Flames danced and crackled inside the hearth, casting flickering shadows on the walls. Three stockings hung from the mantle, their embroidered names catching the firelight: Andrew, Emma, and Lily.

The sight of the third stocking brought a genuine smile to Emma's lips. Though she hadn't met Andrew's girlfriend yet, Lily's presence was evident in the thoughtful holiday touches throughout the room. Her eyes landed on the nativity scene beside the tree—the same one their parents had displayed every Christmas before passing it on to Andrew when they downsized. The familiar figures stood together like a timeless scene, a lasting reminder of faith and family.

The carved figures brought memories of her parents, Clark and Penny, now happily retired in their cabin further up in the mountains of Laurel Ridge. Their sister Harper lived nearby too, running the local animal shelter.

"Lily decorated," Andrew said, hanging his coat on a peg by the door. "I can't take credit for any of this Pinterest-worthy charm."

"Figures," Emma teased, sinking into the corner of the sofa. "I can see the touch of a real pro decorator in every corner of this place."

He disappeared into the kitchen, returning moments later with two steaming mugs. "Hot cocoa, just like old times," he said, passing one to her. "And to think you used to mock my cocoa-making skills."

"Because you used to burn it," she replied, wrapping both hands around the warm ceramic. The rich chocolate aroma transported her back to simpler days, when her greatest worry was whether Santa would bring the porcelain doll she'd circled in every catalog.

"So," she began, her voice catching slightly. "How's life as Laurel Ridge's newest spiritual guide?"

Andrew settled into the armchair across from her, blowing steam from his mug. "Good. I'm finding my footing since Eli retired. Though I still catch myself wanting to check with him before making decisions."

"I always knew you would make a fine pastor," Emma said softly.

His eyes met hers, gentle but searching. "How do you feel about moving back here? I think you made the right call, even if it was sudden. The elementary school is thrilled to have you taking over for Clair as their school nurse."

Emma stirred her cocoa, watching the thin trails of steam curl upward like questions without answers. The accident flashed through her mind—screeching tires, blinding lights, then nothing but hospital walls and emptiness. She forced a smile, though her throat tightened. "It's... overwhelming. Selling everything in Pittsburgh, leaving the hospital, taking the school position here—it's a lot. On the drive down, it really hit me how much has changed in just a few weeks. The past year..." She paused, struggling to find the words. "I came back for a fresh start, to be closer to family, to heal somehow. But now that I'm here, it feels so real. Seventeen years of life in Pittsburgh, and all I have left fits in that trailer outside. I feel lost, but excited too, in a way. Ready to start again on my terms." Her voice softened. "I miss Rhett. Since he died, there's been this... space inside me that nothing seems to fill."

"Grief has no timeline," Andrew said, his voice steady and warm. "Healing isn't a solo journey, Em. You need people. Family. This town? It's full of folks who've known you since you were trading stickers on the playground. You'll see."

She looked up at him, grateful for his quiet faith in both the world and her resilience. The ache in her chest remained, sharp as the winter wind, but his words offered a glimmer of comfort.

"Besides," he added, his eyes twinkling, "the town's already buzzing about your return. I should start taking reservations for your welcome-home tour."

"Oh no," Emma groaned. "I'm going to be the headline at Martha's Diner, aren't I?"

"That place makes the local news channel look slow. By lunchtime tomorrow, even Earl Smith at the hardware store will swear he predicted your return months ago."

The laugh that bubbled up surprised her—genuine and free, like releasing a breath she'd held too long.

Andrew's grin widened. "And speaking of predictable town talk... You know Mark Thompson teaches fourth grade at the elementary school... just thought you should know."

Emma's laughter faltered. "Mark?" The name tugged at a thread she'd carefully tied off years ago, one she'd tried to forget existed. Their breakup hadn't been clean.

She shook her head. "No, I didn't know that. I'm not exactly up on the Laurel Ridge social registry anymore."

Andrew's eyebrow lifted, but he didn't press. "Well, the rumor mill awaits. If there's one thing this town loves, it's a potential reconciliation story."

"Let's not add kindling to that particular fire," Emma said firmly. "I need to figure out who I am now before I think about... becoming involved with anyone. And when I do, I can't imagine it being Mark Thompson."

"Got it," Andrew said, then, shifting the topic, added, "Your first day at the school is this Friday, right?"

"Yes," Emma replied, "that gives me the next two days to settle in before I start. I'm planning to start looking right away for either a house to buy or maybe an apartment or a small home to rent."

Her brother nodded, tilting his head slightly as he studied her in the warm radiance of the firelight. "Take your time. There's no rush. You can stay as long as you'd like. I've got plenty of space, and honestly, it'll be nice to have some company. It gets pretty quiet living here alone."

"Thanks, I just don't want to overstay my welcome," Emma said. "How's Lily doing?"

Lily Reynolds, Andrew's girlfriend, was in the midst of packing up her life as well. She was subletting her Manhattan apartment and wrapping up a few last-minute wedding planning jobs she had committed to. Soon, she would be moving to Laurel Ridge to be closer to Andrew and to launch her graphic design business.

"She's doing really well. She was just here last weekend and is planning to come back in a couple of weeks," Andrew said. "I'm excited for you to meet her. You will love her."

"Has she found an apartment around here yet?" Emma asked.

"She's found a few options and is seriously considering one that Leslie Williams will have available in January, right above her flower shop," Andrew said.

"That's great! I bet she's really excited about the move," Emma replied.

"Yes, she's thrilled. She's planning to run her graphic design business from home and can't wait to be done with her wedding planning job. Just like you, she's going to sell almost everything and bring only the essentials when it's time to move," Andrew said.

"How are Mom, Dad, and Harper? I haven't had a chance to talk to them in the last couple of weeks—I've just been so busy," Emma said.

"Speaking of them, we should probably give them a call to let them know you arrived safely. Mom and Dad are doing well and thoroughly enjoying retirement. Mom's been quilting non-stop, and Dad's been reading a lot. He's also working on a set of plans to build a barn this spring. Harper's doing great, as busy as ever with her animal shelter," Andrew said.

"I'll text them in a bit to let them know I've arrived. So, what do you have planned for tomorrow?" Emma asked.

"My schedule is wide open. I cleared my entire day tomorrow so I can help you unpack the trailer and return it to the U-Haul facility. I've even made space in the garage for you to store your things," Andrew said. "I was thinking we should start the day with breakfast at the diner with the rest of the family. I know Martha's excited to see you again, too."

"Sounds good," Emma said. "I hate to be a downer, but I'm absolutely exhausted from traveling all day. Would you mind if I called it a night?"

"No, not at all. Let's take your bags up to your room," Andrew said as they both got up to retrieve Emma's luggage.

Andrew and Emma climbed the stairs to the upper floor, where Andrew led Emma to the room he had prepared for her. The bedroom was decorated in lovely shades of warm neutral colors, had a private bathroom and a spacious walk-in closet. As they stepped into the softly lit space, the faint scent of a cranberry candle filled the air. After placing Emma's luggage down, they hugged each other and said goodnight, then Andrew quietly left the room, pulling the door shut behind him.

Kneeling beside her suitcase, she pulled out a silver frame—her and Rhett, captured in a moment of pure joy just months before the accident. His smile still made her heart skip, his arms forever frozen around her in an embrace she'd never feel again. Her finger traced his face through the glass as tears threatened to fall.

"I don't know if I'm ready for all this," she whispered to the silence, her voice thick with emotion. "But I'll try. I'll keep moving forward, build something new here. That's what you'd want."

After changing into pajamas, Emma knelt beside the bed, the quiet broken only by the wind against the windows and the distant pop of firewood downstairs.

"Lord," she prayed, her whispered words trembling in the stillness, "I don't understand Your plan for me yet. I thought coming home would help me heal, help things make sense in life again. I need to start over and end this constant cycle of feeling like I am lost. I'm tired of feeling like I'm floating around without a purpose. It's time for a change, and I'm ready to turn the page and start a new chapter in my life. I need Your strength to find my way through this. Please grant me the courage to rebuild if that's Your will for me. Help me trust in Your guidance, even when the path ahead feels dark."

She paused, letting her fears rise to the surface like leaves in a stream.

"Please... help me find peace again," she finished, her voice barely audible. "Let me trust in the journey You've prepared, seeing each new day as a step toward hope."

As she slipped beneath the covers, her gaze drifted to the window, where snow continued its silent dance in the moonlight. Laurel Ridge stretched before her—a tapestry of past and future, challenges and possibilities.

The wind whispered against the glass, a gentle reminder that tomorrow would bring its own mercies, and its own chances to begin again.

Chapter 2

The winter winds whipped past Mark Thompson's rustic cabin as he sat at his kitchen table, watching the sunset paint the snow-covered landscape in soft hues of pink and gold. The quiet moment was a stark contrast to the lively car ride home from school, where Olivia's cheerful voice had filled every second with tales of second-grade adventures and Christmas craft mishaps.

His gaze drifted to the empty chair across the table, where Maggie used to sit. Four years had passed since cancer claimed her, yet occasionally the weight of her absence still pressed against his chest like a physical thing. If it hadn't been for Olivia—his bright-eyed, perpetually optimistic seven-year-old daughter—he might have gotten lost in that darkness. Instead, her need for him had become his anchor, her infectious laughter a daily reminder that joy could exist even amid loss.

Mark stood, stretching tired muscles from a long day of teaching. His eyes swept across the room, taking in the subtle touches of Christmas that he and Olivia had managed to create handmade garland crafted during last weekend's visit with his Grandma Claire, battery-operated candles casting a soft light from the mantle, and Olivia's latest artistic masterpiece—a glitter-covered ornament that caught the fading light of day.

A bittersweet smile tugged at his lips. Maggie would have loved this—the way Olivia threw herself into the holiday spirit with complete abandon. Maggie had always been the one who transformed their home into a wonderland of twinkling lights and homemade decorations, filling every corner with the scent of freshly baked cookies and the sound of Christmas carols.

The wooden stairs creaked softly beneath his feet as he climbed to wake Olivia from her after-school nap. The hinges of Olivia's door creaked as he pushed it open.

Golden rays of the setting sun filtered through her window, casting warm patterns across her sleeping form. "Peanut," he called softly. His daughter's curls peeked out from beneath her blanket, one small fist clutching her pillow with determined strength.

A sleepy, "Daddy?" emerged from the cocoon of blankets, followed by the slow blink of brown eyes that never failed to remind him of Maggie.

"Time to get up, sweetheart. We don't want to be late for dinner at Grandma and Pop's house." Mark settled on the edge of her bed, watching as she fought against wakefulness with the dramatic flair only a seven-year-old could muster.

"Just five more minutes," Olivia pleaded, burrowing deeper under her quilt—the same one she'd dragged everywhere since infancy.

Mark chuckled. "I already gave you five minutes. And ten extra." He gently tugged the quilt down, revealing her lightly freckled face and sleep-flushed cheeks.

A giggle escaped her as she admitted defeat, stretching her arms overhead with exaggerated effort. "Okay, okay, I'm awake," she mumbled, the words still fuzzy with sleep as she swung her legs over the side of the bed.

The transformation from sleepy child to bouncing ball of energy happened in the space of a heartbeat. Before Mark could blink, Olivia was racing down the hallway, her footsteps creating a joyful percussion against the wooden floors. These were the moments that reminded him how beautiful life could be—messy and unpredictable at times, but filled with these precious pockets of pure joy.

Snow crunched beneath their boots as they made their way down the familiar path to his grandparents' home, their breath rising in crystalline clouds against the darkening sky. Warm light spilled from the windows of Eli and Claire's home.

The aroma of roasted chicken and sweet potatoes wrapped around them like a welcome embrace as they approached the front porch. Olivia's energy, already at full force, somehow managed to increase. "I smell dinner!" she exclaimed, darting ahead before Mark could remind her about wiping her boots.

Claire Thompson opened the door, her familiar smile crinkling the corners of her eyes. "Well, look who's here!" she greeted them warmly, opening her arms to catch Olivia in a hug.

"Gigi, can I help with dinner?" Olivia tumbled into her great-grandmother's embrace with characteristic enthusiasm.

"You were born to help with dinner, sweetheart," Claire laughed, leading her toward the kitchen. "The potatoes are waiting for your special touch."

Mark stepped into the warmth of his grandparents' home, letting the familiar scents and sounds wash over him. Eli sat in his favorite armchair in the living room, the muted sounds of a football game providing gentle background noise as he lowered his newspaper with a knowing smile.

"There's the man of the hour," Eli greeted. "How was school today, Mark?"

Following their well-worn routine, Mark settled into his usual seat across from his grandfather. These evening check-ins had become a cornerstone of his life, especially after losing Maggie. "The usual pre-holiday chaos," he admitted with a wry smile. "Had to give the traditional 'focus on your work now, enjoy your Christmas break later' speech today."

Eli's laugh shook his shoulders. "Some things never change, do they? Reminds me of when you were in school."

"At least we knew better than to act up back then," Mark countered. "Detention and extra homework were pretty effective deterrents."

The easy rhythm of their conversation was interrupted by Claire's call from the kitchen, her voice carrying the gentle authority of someone who had spent decades orchestrating family gatherings. "Dinner's ready! And Olivia's already improving my recipes, Mark."

"Of course she is," Mark called back, sharing an amused look with his grandfather.

Around the dinner table, they joined hands for grace, their circle complete and strong. Eli's prayer of thanksgiving resonated through the room, acknowledging their blessings and the bonds of family that held them together. As soon as the final "Amen" was whispered, Olivia launched into her daily report with characteristic enthusiasm.

"Daddy, guess what?" She barely paused between spoonfuls of mashed potatoes. "Mrs. Davis said I make the best glitter snowflakes in the whole class! And remember, we need to get our Christmas tree soon—you promised!" It was her third reminder that week, each one delivered with increasing excitement.

Mark's eyes crinkled with affection. "We'll find the perfect tree soon, Liv. I haven't forgotten."

Claire passed the green beans, her eyes twinkling. "Your daddy was just like you at your age, Olivia. Always had to have the biggest Christmas tree and wanted it as soon as the Thanksgiving holiday was finished." She winked at her great-granddaughter. "I have a feeling this year's tree will be extra special."

"Big trees are the best," Olivia declared, her legs swinging beneath the table as she stabbed a carrot with determined precision. "We need lots of room for all our decorations."

Eli leaned back in his chair, amusement dancing in his eyes. "Might need some help with that perfect tree this year, Mark. You're not as young as you used to be."

"I'll manage just fine, thanks, Pops," Mark retorted, grinning over his cup of coffee.

The evening settled softly around them as Olivia's animated chatter filled the air. Mark listened to her stories about glitter mishaps and lunchtime childhood drama, his heart full of the simple blessing of these family dinners. Despite everything life had thrown at them, moments like these reminded him of how much good remained.

Later, as they walked home under a canopy of stars, Olivia's mitten'd hand tucked safely in his, Mark felt a deep sense of peace. The snow crunched beneath their boots, and Olivia's endless stream of conversation ("...and Mrs. Davis said we can bring our favorite stuffed animal tomorrow!") drifted up into the night air like a joyful prayer.

At home, the bedtime routine unfolded with familiar comfort. Olivia barely managed to stay awake through changing into her pajamas, her earlier energy finally depleted. As Mark tucked her under her quilt, she managed one last sleepy reminder: "Don't forget about our Christmas tree, Daddy..."

"Never," he promised, pressing a kiss to her forehead. "Sweet dreams, Olivia."

In the quiet of the evening, Mark sat at the dining room table, a stack of fourth-grade homework assignments waiting for his attention. But his thoughts drifted instead to memories of that first Christmas with Maggie and Olivia when their little girl was just months old. He could still picture it perfectly: the snow-laden branches outside their window, the crackling fireplace, the mingled scents of evergreen and sugar cookies.

Olivia had been so tiny then, fast asleep in his arms in her red footie pajamas, a miniature Santa hat sliding off her downy head. The depth of love he'd felt in that moment—watching Maggie hum carols as she decorated their tree, their newborn daughter sleeping peacefully against his chest—had been almost overwhelming.

That year, Maggie had hand-painted a wooden heart ornament with Olivia's name, adding it to their collection with such tender care. He remembered the way she'd looked at him across the room, her face glowing with a joy that seemed to radiate from within. That Christmas Eve, they'd sat together by the tree, Olivia sleeping between them on a soft blanket, their fingers intertwined. No words needed to express the perfect contentment of that moment.

These memories no longer carried the sharp edge of grief they once had. Instead, they felt like a gentle reminder of the love that had helped shape him, that continued to shape his life through Olivia. Maggie's absence had become like a familiar song playing softly in the background of their lives—always there, but no longer overwhelming.

Bowing his head, Mark offered a quiet prayer of gratitude. "Lord, thank you for these blessings—for Olivia, for family, for the gift of memory and love. Guide us forward on whatever path You've prepared, knowing that Your plan is perfect, even when we can't see the whole picture."

The snow continued to fall outside, each flake a reminder that even in the midst of winter, new beauty was constantly being created. Tomorrow would bring its own challenges and joys, but for now, in the quiet of this moment, Mark felt the deep assurance that they were exactly where they needed to be.

Chapter 3

As Emma and Andrew entered the cozy atmosphere of Martha's Diner, the bell above the door jingled. Bacon, coffee, and fresh pancakes filled the air with their delicious scent. The diner was just as Emma remembered it. The gleaming black-and-white checkered floors and red vinyl booths were illuminated by the festive glow of Christmas lights.

Andrew nudged her playfully. "Well, here you are, back in the heart of Laurel Ridge."

Emma smiled. She took a deep breath, allowing herself to savor the sense of nostalgia that washed over her. Coming back to Laurel Ridge was supposed to feel comforting, and in many ways, it did. Yet, deep down, there were fragments of herself she didn't know how to gather or where exactly they fit.

Still, there was the welcoming warmth of her brother next to her, and ahead—her family, their eyes lighting up as soon as they spotted her. Penny Whitman—their mother—was out of the booth within seconds, her arms reaching for Emma as she approached.

"There's my girl!" Penny's voice was full of joy, and the next thing Emma knew, she was wrapped in the familiar, comforting embrace of her mother.

Clark, their father, stood nearby, his kind eyes crinkling behind his wire-rimmed glasses. When Emma turned to him, his hug was strong and steady—just like him. "Good to have you back where you belong, Em," he murmured.

Harper, their spirited youngest sibling, threw an arm around Emma's shoulder with a grin. "Well, it's about time you got back. Someone has to keep Andrew in line, and that's a full-time job."

Emma laughed. "Don't worry. I'm on it."

As she took her seat, she felt loved and knew she had made the right decision to come back home. The diner activity hummed quietly around them—customers spoke with one another across tables, the clatter of dishes was punctuated by soft laughter, and somewhere in the background, a holiday tune played softly through the air.

Martha Kincaid appeared from the kitchen like a force of nature, her silver hair escaping its neat bun and her apron dusted with flour. Her eyes sparkled with the same mischief that had always made her diner feel more like a second home than a business.

"Well, if it isn't Emma Whitman back from the big city!" Martha's cheerful, slightly teasing voice rang out.

Emma couldn't help but grin at her. "Hi, Martha."

"Now don't 'Hi, Martha' me, young lady—" Martha ducked closer, wrapping her arms around Emma in a big, genuine hug before pulling back, "—I thought I'd lost you to Pittsburgh forever!" She winked. "I'm sure glad to have you home again."

Emma laughed. "It's good to be back."

Martha tapped the table lightly with her hand. "Are y'all are ready to order? You're not leavin' this place until you're fed properly. It's what this town runs on: good food and good gossip—and you, dear Emma, are the talk of the day." Martha pointed a playful finger. "Gossip's already spreadin' faster than fresh coffee on a cold morning that you're back."

"Oh, I'm sure of it," Andrew said with a chuckle, glancing at Emma with a knowing look. "She can't hide here, that's for sure."

"Who says I'm hiding?" Emma teased.

Martha jotted down their "usual orders," pleased to know that not much had changed in Emma's food preferences over the years, and scurried off to the kitchen.

Clark leaned across the table, his gray-blue eyes twinkling behind his glasses. "So, Em, how does it feel to be back home? The move back, starting a new job at the school... it's a lot. You ready?"

Emma's lips pressed together thoughtfully. She looked at her father, at her mother's gentle, encouraging expression, at Harper's playfully raised brows, and Andrew's steady presence beside her.

"I'm... excited, but I'd be lying if I said I wasn't nervous, too," Emma admitted.

Penny reached out and placed her hand over Emma's, offering a gentle squeeze. "That's perfectly normal, darling. You've been through a lot. A move like this would feel overwhelming to anyone. But starting fresh, right here at home? That's a blessing."

Harper nodded. "Plus, working at the elementary school? That's gotta feel like a bit of a relief, right? No more long shifts at a big hospital."

Emma nodded. "Yeah, it feels like the right place for me right now. It's like I need calm again in my life—to reset. My job at the hospital and working all the shifts I had been to fill my time... well, I'm honestly looking forward to slowing down some. Clair Thompson left some big shoes for me to fill at the school, but I'm excited to step into that role."

"I have no doubt you'll do just fine," Andrew said, sipping his coffee. "And from what I've been hearing, the school is really excited to have you on board. While Clair was a legend in her own right, you'll come up with your own way of doing things—and the kids will love you as well."

Clark rubbed his hands together like he was warming them up, along with the conversation. "Have you got any thoughts or ideas about housing? I'd imagine the parsonage upstairs isn't the long-term plan, right?"

Emma glanced slowly around the table, hesitating for a moment. She loved her family, and having Andrew nearby was comforting, but eventually, she'd need her own space. "I've been thinking about it," she answered. "I don't want to make any rash decisions, though, you know? I want to find a place that feels right for me. Something small... cozy, maybe even a fixer-upper. I'd really rather find a home I can buy, but I'll settle on renting something if I need to."

Harper leaned back in her chair with an expressive grin. "Well, if you want help looking, you know I'll gladly be your real estate sidekick. I've heard of a few places that might be opening up soon."

Penny chimed in eagerly. "Oh, there are some lovely little houses near the school, Emma—you know the neighborhood up on Walnut Street? Some of the homes there might be just what you're looking for. I can drive you by them later if you like. And of course," she smiled knowingly, "Martha's always got her ear to the ground. We'll ask her before we leave."

Andrew chuckled, flashing Emma a wink. "Look out, you're going to have half the town showing you houses or apartments by Friday. Word travels faster than a cold front around here."

Emma laughed, but appreciated the support. "I think I'll take things a little slow. I haven't even unpacked my things in your spare room, Andrew."

"Well," Martha's voice interjected as she returned with a tray full of steaming plates, "sounds like you've already got a whole realtor team lined up—you'll be settled into a cozy little place of your own before you know it. And if anyone knows of any hidden gems, it's probably me." With a dramatic pause, she added, "For the record, Emma, I've got my eye on an adorable cottage near the tree farm. I'm thinking it may be perfect for you. Maybe after your pancakes, we can talk."

The entire family chuckled at the idea of Martha tucking Emma under her wing as a homebuyer. It was exactly what Emma envisioned, though—the spirit of Laurel Ridge in full swing, with the generous, well-meaning neighbors eager to make her transition smooth.

Emma grinned at Martha. "I might just take you up on that."

Martha patted her back fondly before nodding toward the table, laden with home style plates of eggs, bacon, toast, and pancakes. "Now eat up! Full bellies make life easier."

As the family started to dig into their meals, conversation flowed as naturally as ever. Harper nudged Emma's elbow, making her look up mid-bite.

"So, with you holding court as the new school nurse, have you thought about what all that means for your new social life?" Harper shot her a teasing grin.

Emma raised an eyebrow playfully. "Harper. Please."

"Oh," Andrew jumped in, shaking his head with a chuckle, "it's only been a day, and already the speculation begins." He winked across the table at Emma.

"Hey," Emma said, holding up a hand playfully, but feeling a brief, flickering tension deep in her chest, "I came home to figure out my next steps in life, not to expand my social life."

"So," Penny began, her voice gently probing as she sipped her coffee, "Wendy and Leah are thrilled you've moved back. Any plans to reconnect with them soon?"

Emma's thoughts drifted to her two best friends from childhood, memories of their shared laughter, inside jokes, and the countless hours they'd spent together resurfacing. Wendy, with her easygoing warmth and infectious giggle, had always been the steady one—rooted in her family farm, loyal to the core. And Leah, ever the adventurer, with a spark of mischief in her eyes and boundless energy to match, had made every day feel like a spontaneous joyride. It had been over a decade since they'd last been truly close, and time had a way of making even the strongest friendships feel fragile. Life had taken them on different paths, and though they'd kept in touch somewhat, there was a distance between them now. Not one created by any sort of falling out, but by the natural drift that comes with time, jobs, and the inevitable complexities of adulthood.

Still, the thought of reconnecting with them brought a glimmer of hope, like the possibility of restoring a piece of herself. Maybe Wendy's grounded presence and Leah's contagious enthusiasm was exactly what she needed.

"Honestly, I've been thinking about it," Emma admitted, swirling her mug of coffee in front of her as if it might provide her with clearer thoughts. "I could definitely use some reconnecting. It's just... I've been away for so long, you know. I don't even know where to start."

Penny's eyes softened as she leaned in, brushing back a few strands of her silver-blonde hair. "Sweetheart, true friendships don't fade. Wendy and Leah have been looking forward to you coming home. I ran into Wendy last week at the Farmstead Store, and all she could talk about was how wonderful it'll be to have you around again."

Emma smiled at the thought of Wendy still rushing around her orchard and managing her cozy little store. "I'll give them a call soon," Emma said.

Andrew, seated beside her and listening quietly, cleared his throat, his voice gentle when he spoke. "Em, Wendy and Leah are still the same remarkable people they've always been."

Clark chimed in with his reassuring tone, "You know Emma, think of it this way too. You're not the same person you were when you left, and neither are they. People change, but that doesn't mean good friendships can't grow again... Just differently. You come together with new experiences, new perspectives. Sometimes," his smile widened, "that makes things even better."

The truth in her father's words settled over Emma. She hadn't really thought about it that way. Perhaps she was holding on too tightly to the past—the version of herself she used to be, the version of her friendships that had been so deeply tied to who she once was. Maybe Wendy and Leah weren't expecting her to be the same girl who left for nursing school all those years ago. Maybe they weren't the same people, either. She had to give herself—and them—the grace to embrace whatever this new chapter of their friendship might look like.

"I suppose I have been overthinking it," Emma mused, her gaze drifting out the diner's frosted windows to the snow-covered world outside. "It'll be good to catch up. I just... I don't want them to see me as some kind of stranger."

Penny's voice was soft, but full of affection. "Oh, Emma, you could never be a stranger to them! The three of you have too much history for that. And remember, they understand what you've been through."

Harper leaned across the table, her hazel eyes glinting with playful resolve. "Well, if you're too hesitant, we might have to stage an intervention to make it happen. I bet Leah's still into spontaneous hangouts," she teased with a grin. "You know, the kind where she just appears at your door, fully expecting you to drop everything and come join her in one of her crazy plans, or—what did she used to say? Oh, right—'seize the day!' I wouldn't put it past her to rope you into some grand catch-up adventure."

Emma chuckled, remembering Leah's boundless enthusiasm for living life to the fullest. "Yeah, you're probably right. I can already picture her standing outside, throwing pebbles at my window, begging me to join her for something crazy."

Andrew smiled knowingly. "Exactly. And Wendy? She'll most likely lure you to the farm with a basket of fresh-baked apple scones or buttered rosemary bread. That's how they'll get you—through your love of carbs."

Emma laughed. "Okay, okay. You've convinced me. I'll reach out to them soon."

"Atta girl," Clark said with a proud smile. "You're already making strides. A step at a time, right?"

Chapter 4

The December wind whistled through the bare trees, sending spirals of powdery snow dancing across Andrew's driveway as Emma lifted another cardboard box from the cargo trailer. This one, labeled "kitchen essentials" in her neat handwriting.

"Almost there." Andrew called out, his breath visible in the crisp morning air. "Once we've got everything unloaded, we can head inside where it's warm. Though, fair warning–" he shot her a guilty grin, "We should probably move those boxes of extra Christmas decorations I still have stacked in your room."

Emma raised an eyebrow. "Oh, you mean the boxes that line one entire wall of the room?"

"I'm clearly the worst brother in the history of brothers," Andrew replied with an exaggerated sigh, as he set a box down in the garage. "Though, in my defense, I did manage to clear out most of my books from the closet."

"Most?" Emma laughed, her breath forming delicate clouds in the frigid air. She turned back toward the trailer, mentally calculating the remaining boxes. At this pace, they'd be done in twenty minutes or so.

The low rumble of an approaching vehicle caught her attention just as she reached for another box. Tires crunched softly over the snow-packed driveway, and a dark blue truck wound its way toward them. Emma's heart skipped a beat as she caught sight of two faces through the windshield, both wearing grins as bright as the surrounding snow.

"Wendy and Leah," she whispered, an unexpected lump forming in her throat. Seventeen years of memories rushed back instantly—summer nights spent stargazing, spontaneous adventures, shared dreams whispered over cups of hot chocolate.

Andrew glanced up from where he'd been arranging boxes in the garage, a knowing smile spreading across his face. "Well, would you look at that—the cavalry's arrived!"

The truck came to a gentle stop, and before the engine had fully quieted, both doors flew open. Wendy appeared first, her long brown hair tucked beneath a hand-knitted hat. Her eyes were bright with tears as she practically flew across the snowy drive.

"Oh my goodness, it's really you!" Wendy's voice cracked with emotion as she reached for Emma. "Emma Whitman, in the very snow-frosted flesh. You're actually here!"

"Emma!" Leah's voice rang out like a bell as she bounded from the passenger side, her signature auburn curls escaping from beneath a chunky wool cap. She hadn't changed a bit—same sparkle in her eyes, same boundless energy that had always made life more adventurous. "It's really happening! Our girl is back!"

Before Emma could respond, she found herself sandwiched between her two oldest friends in the kind of hug that somehow manages to squeeze out every worry and doubt.

"I've missed you both so much," Emma managed through happy tears, holding them tight. The weight of the past few weeks seemed to lift a little in their embrace.

Leah pulled back first, her eyes dancing as she planted her hands on her hips in a stance Emma remembered from countless teenage negotiations. "We thought we'd lost you forever to the big city! Though I have to say, your timing is perfect—you've arrived just in time for the Winter Festival and the Christmas play at church, which, by the way... we need more volunteers."

Emma laughed, wiping her eyes. "Some things never change, do they? Still trying to rope me into your schemes?"

"Always!" Leah declared proudly. "And this time you can't escape—you're stuck here with us now forever. We won't let you leave again."

"Amen to that," Wendy added, squeezing Emma's hand. "Laurel Ridge hasn't been the same without you."

From the garage, Andrew cleared his throat dramatically with a grin. "Hey, reunion committee! If you're done with the touching moment, there are still a few boxes that need moving. Unless you'd rather stand out here freezing while Emma's coffee maker gets frostbite?"

"Heaven forbid!" Leah gasped in mock horror, already marching toward the trailer. "Come on, girls—like the old days. Teamwork makes the dream work!"

"Some catchphrases should stay in high school," Wendy groaned, but she was smiling as she followed Leah's lead.

The next few minutes flew by in a flurry of activity and laughter. Stories flowed as freely as their visible breath in the cold air—Wendy's latest orchard expansion plans, Leah's ideas to add another line of specialty gifts to what the Farmstead Store offered, the time Andrew had accidentally locked himself out of the church parsonage during last month's snowstorm. It was as if the years apart dissolved with each shared laugh and remembered inside joke.

Between the four of them, the remaining boxes soon found their way into the garage.

"Now that we've successfully prevented Emma's kitchen supplies from becoming ice sculptures, I vote we move this party inside," Andrew announced, rubbing his hands together vigorously. "I've got coffee, and I think there might even be some of Mom's Christmas cookies left.

"Oh, thank goodness," Leah breathed, shivering with perhaps a touch more drama than necessary. "I can't feel my toes anymore!"

Wendy rolled her eyes. "Please—you went skiing in worse weather than this just last week!" She gave Leah a playful nudge.

As they filed into the warmth of Andrew's kitchen, their laughter echoed off the walls.

"Oh, sweet mercy, this feels absolutely heavenly in here," Leah sighed dramatically, tugging off her knitted hat. Her auburn curls sprang free in their characteristic wild abandon.

"It seems colder than usual for this time of year," Wendy added, unwinding her scarf. "Grandma says it's the coldest December we've had in years."

The warmth of Andrew's kitchen embraced them like an old friend, melting away the winter chill and any lingering awkwardness that seventeen years apart might have created. Steam rose from the coffeemaker as Andrew worked his magic at the counter.

"The famous Whitman coffee service is about to commence," Andrew announced with a flourish, carrying over a tray laden with mugs and a plate of snickerdoodle cookies. "Still remember how everyone takes their coffee, Em?"

Emma smiled, thinking back to the days she waitressed at the local coffee shop as a teenager. "Let's see... Wendy takes hers with just a splash of cream, Leah drowns hers in both cream and sugar, and you," she pointed at her brother, "drink it black."

"Some things never change," Wendy laughed.

The conversation began to flow as naturally as the steam rising from their cups. The kitchen filled with the comfortable hum of voices and laughter, creating a cocoon of warmth against the winter day outside. Through the window, snow had begun to fall again, fat flakes drifting lazily past the glass, but inside, memories were falling just as softly, blanketing them in shared history.

"Remember the summer dance at the recreation hall?" Leah asked, her eyes sparkling with mischief. "The one where Emma convinced us all to perform that ridiculous dance routine?"

"Oh no," Emma groaned, but she was already laughing. "In my defense, I thought the Macarena was making a comeback."

"Spoiler alert—it wasn't," Wendy deadpanned, then dissolved into giggles. "Though I have to say, watching Pastor Eli try to follow along was worth every mortifying moment."

"But nothing," Leah declared, "absolutely nothing tops the Great Sledding Incident." She leaned forward, her eyes gleaming. "Emma, I still maintain that was your finest moment."

Emma nearly choked on her coffee. "My finest moment? I ended up in a cast for six weeks! The entire town banned sledding competitions because of us!"

"Because of me, you mean," Leah corrected proudly. "I still say that hill behind the school was perfectly safe. You just didn't commit to cardboard sled technology."

"Oh, I committed alright," Emma laughed, shaking her head at the memory. "I committed to breaking my arm in two places and giving poor Clair Thompson a heart attack when she came to help me at the bottom of that hill."

"Character building!" Leah insisted, waving a cookie for emphasis. "Tell me that experience didn't prepare you for life's other challenges. I mean, look at you now—a seasoned nurse who can handle anything!"

"School nurse now," Emma corrected.

Wendy reached across the table and squeezed her hand. "And you're going to be wonderful at it. Those kids are lucky to have someone who understands both medical emergencies and the importance of proper sledding technique."

"Though, maybe don't share the cardboard sled story with any of the kids," Andrew suggested, earning a playful swat from Emma.

The laughter that followed felt like a warm embrace. These were the people who had helped shape her faith, who had prayed with her through her first heartbreak, who had celebrated her acceptance to nursing school even while knowing it would take her away from them. Looking at their familiar faces now, Emma realized that coming home wasn't just about starting over—it was about remembering who she had been and discovering who she could still become.

"I've missed this," she admitted, her voice thick with emotion. "I've missed you all so much."

"Well, get used to having us around," Leah declared, reaching for another cookie. "Because now that you're back, we're not letting you go again. Right, Wendy?"

"Right," Wendy agreed. "Though maybe we'll skip the death-defying sledding adventures this time around."

"Speak for yourself," Leah protested with a wink. "I've got some great ideas for the Winter Festival."

"Speaking of the Winter Festival... Emma, you have no idea how amazing it's going to be this year. We've got so many plans—the whole town's been buzzing about it for weeks!" Wendy said.

The mention of the Winter Festival sent a warm rush of memories through Emma's mind, as vivid as if they'd happened yesterday. She could almost smell the gingerbread and hot chocolate, and hear the cheerful chaos of children and adults alike having fun.

The festival had always been one of her favorite parts of Christmas in Laurel Ridge. There was something special about the way it brought everyone together, creating moments of wonder not just for the children, but for the whole community. It was about more than just the events and activities—it was about faith, family, and the kind of love that made a small-town feel like one big family.

"I remember how exciting the festival was," Emma said. "It always felt like Christmas itself lived right here in Laurel Ridge."

Wendy's eyes lit up. "Oh, it still does! If anything, it's gotten even bigger since you left. We've got a Christmas tree lighting ceremony planned, ice skating, a snowman-building contest, and—" she leaned in with a mischievous grin, "—a new hot cocoa competition. I still think Mrs. Houser's putting something extra in hers, though she'll never admit it."

Leah shook her head, laughing. "You mean she isn't giving away her 'secret recipe'? Shocking."

Andrew leaned back with an amused sigh. "You all realize, of course, that the highlight of the Winter Festival is the children's Christmas play."

"You should come, Emma. Who could resist a bunch of adorable kids dressed up as sheep and angels?" Leah said.

"I'll probably go to both," Emma said, her head nodding as Leah's excitement grew.

"And how about volunteering?" Wendy pressed with a playful smirk. "I mean, if there's any way to get you squarely back into the fold of Laurel Ridge, it's probably corralling a bunch of kids in shepherd costumes for the play, right?"

Emma grinned, pretending to think it over. "Fine, but if I end up wrangling Joseph and the wise men, I'm calling in reinforcements."

Leah's hand shot up, earning a surprised look from Wendy. "Consider me your backup! It's time someone else took on the sheep-herding."

They shared a moment of comfortable laughter, the kind that came from years of history and trust, their warmth melting the edges of time that had kept them apart.

The conversation slowly began to wind down, boots shuffled back on, and scarves were wrapped tightly as Leah and Wendy prepared to head out into the snow-dusted world again.

"You know where to find us," Wendy smiled, stepping out onto the porch and pulling her hat down to cover her ears.

"And don't be a stranger, okay?" Leah added, her voice fading into the winter wind.

"I won't let her." Andrew called after them, closing the door behind the gusts of snow as they retreated to their truck, leaving Emma with an empty coffee mug and an awfully full heart.

Chapter 5

Mark Thompson let the engine of his pickup truck hum to silence as he parked in his driveway. The falling snow swirled gently, illuminated by the late afternoon sunlight.

"Daddy, let's go!" came the cheerful demand from the back seat.

Mark chuckled as he glanced in the rearview mirror at Olivia, her little face flushed with excitement beneath a pink knitted hat. She clutched her lunchbox in one mitten'd hand, her book bag sitting beside her.

"Coming, Olivia," he replied, his tone gently teasing as he tugged his gloves on. He couldn't deny the spark of joy she brought into every corner of his life, filling his life with laughter where silence might have reigned. No matter how long the day, no matter how heavy his thoughts, Olivia had a way of making everything seem brighter.

He stepped into the crisp winter air, the frosty breeze nipping at his cheeks as he opened the back door of the truck. Olivia hopped out, her small boots crunching in the snow. With her backpack slung over one shoulder and lunchbox swinging in hand, she darted to the house, leaving tiny footprints along the path that led to the front door. Her giggles echoed through the otherwise still woods surrounding their cabin.

"Watch your step, Liv," he called after her. His daughter had an energy and fearlessness about life that he envied. She darted up to the door, hopping from stone to stone along the snow covered front walk, while Mark plodded along behind—his pace careful, a little slower.

By the time he reached the door, Olivia was already inside, talking a mile a minute about her day. "And the Winter Festival is coming soon! Mrs. Davis says she's going to dress like an elf that day!"

Mark slipped out of his boots and shrugged off his coat, hanging it on the hook near the door.

Olivia plopped down at the dining room table. She started neatly arranging her homework into tidy piles. When she looked up, her eyes landed on a plate of sugar cookies in the middle of the table. Her face lit up with delight. Without hesitation, she hopped down from her chair and grabbed the plate, her small hands lifting it triumphantly as she turned to Mark, who had just walked into the room. "Look, Daddy. Gigi must've brought these for us."

"Your Great-Grandma must have dropped them off today while we were at school. But remember—just one cookie, then straight to your homework," Mark said, flashing a playful grin.

Olivia groaned in exaggerated dismay.

Mark took his usual seat across from Olivia, laying out his work with an easy familiarity. From his well-worn backpack, he pulled out a stack of papers, arranging them on the table. Spelling tests awaited grading, along with a folder of student worksheets. The daily grind—a rhythm he'd fallen into with crisp precision as a single dad—unfolded like clockwork.

But as much as quiet moments like these centered him, Mark's mind started wandering—as it had all day—to Emma Whitman.

He had overheard the chatter in the teacher's lounge that day—snippets of conversation surrounding the arrival of the new school nurse.

"Daddy?" Olivia's voice pulled him from his reverie. She sat up a little straighter, a frown furrowing her brow. "Are you okay?"

Mark blinked, offering a sheepish grin. "Yeah, Liv. Just a little distracted today, that's all."

"Can I have another cookie?" Olivia asked, her mischievous smile already in place, clearly angling for a distraction of her own.

He laughed, shaking his head as he pushed the stack of tests aside. "Alright...you can have another."

Olivia leaped from her chair with the exuberance only a seven-year-old could have, retrieving two cookies and plopping one down in front of her father before returning to her seat. He absently took a bite as he gathered his thoughts, but the sound of a soft knock at the door quickly diverted them once again.

The door creaked open, and Clair's familiar silhouette appeared in the doorway, framed by the light of the snow-covered evening. Olivia leaped from her chair once again, rushing to greet her great-grandmother.

"Gigi!" she squealed, wrapping her arms around Clair's legs.

"Well, lookie here! My two favorite people," Clair beamed with that ever-present, warm smile, bending down to return Olivia's hug. The snow dusted her coat and scarf, and she looked every bit as welcoming as a grandmother should—a picture of gentle love and kindness.

"Hey, Gram," Mark greeted as he stood from his chair, gesturing her inside.

Clair stepped over the threshold, stamping the snow from her boots. "Hi, honey. I baked another batch of cookies and thought I'd bring you some."

Olivia clapped her hands together, her brown eyes lighting up even brighter as she darted to the kitchen counter to unload another plate of cookies.

Mark grinned, shaking his head. "Now what am I going to do with all these sweets, Gram?"

"Oh, I seem to remember someone who could never get enough sugary sweets when you were Olivia's age," Clair teased, slipping off her coat and hanging it alongside his.

Once settled at the kitchen table, they indulged in steaming mugs of hot cocoa and more freshly baked cookies—a welcome respite from the stack of homework assignments waiting to be graded. The sweet warmth of the cocoa seemed to chase away the day's fatigue.

Clair took a sip of her cocoa. "So, how was school? No candy cane-related emergencies, I hope."

Mark chuckled. "Well, the candy distribution hasn't officially started yet, but we've had more snowball fights in the parking lot during school pickups and drop-offs than anything else."

"I remember," Clair said with a chuckle. "In my days working there, just when you thought you had them under control, they'd find a way to make chaos out of snowflakes."

Mark shook his head, settling back into his chair. "It's been good overall. Busy as always at this time of year. The kids are excited about the upcoming Winter Festival. The teachers are counting down the days to Christmas break just as much as the students."

Clair smiled knowingly. "Rest is important for everyone... including teachers."

Mark nodded, though his gaze wandered absently back to the stack of papers beside him. He tapped it lightly with his finger, lost in thought.

"What about you, Olivia?" Clair asked, her warm gaze shifting to her great-granddaughter. "How's Mrs. Davis? And how's that math unit going?"

Olivia groaned dramatically. "Ugh, math is the worst."

"It'll get easier, sweetie," Clair agreed with a playful grin.

Clair's gaze shifted back to Mark, the soft humor in her expression dimming slightly as she turned more serious. She reached for her cocoa, cradling the cup between her hands before she spoke. "Mark, there's something important I wanted to chat with you about tonight."

Mark glanced at her with lifted brows, his body language instantly shifting, though he kept a veneer of calm. "Something up, Gram?"

Clair pressed her lips into a thin line, her brow furrowing just slightly before continuing. "I just want to be sure you're aware... that Emma Whitman moved back to town."

There it was. The name Mark had been half-avoiding, half-obsessing. He should have known Clair would bring it up soon enough, though.

Mark's throat tightened for a moment, his grip on the cocoa mug in his hands now notably firmer.

"I know," he said after a long pause, his voice quiet yet composed. "I've heard she is back."

Clair studied him closely for a moment, her eyes searching his in that familiar, knowing way only grandmothers had. She set her cocoa down on the table. "How do you feel about that?"

Mark swallowed, taking a deep breath before answering. "I don't know, Gram. Emma and I—" He stopped himself, reaching for words that seemed to scatter before he could grab hold of them. "It's going to be awkward seeing her after all these years."

"And...?" Clair's voice was soft, but there was an unmistakable weight to her question, one that didn't allow for easy dismissal.

"I—" He hesitated, gathering his thoughts with care. His mind whirred, filled with conflicting emotions he hadn't quite made sense of yet. "I walked away from our relationship years ago. It was all my doing," he finally said, his voice not hiding the uncertainty beneath the surface.

Clair reached across the table, her hand resting gently atop his clenched fist. "I understand why you made the choices you made, Mark. But God has a way of working things out in ways we can't always understand, especially when it comes to love. And Emma..." Clair paused, choosing her words carefully. "I don't think you ever really stopped loving her."

Mark flinched inwardly, unsure if he was ready to confront the feelings that the statement stirred.

"You think so?" His voice cracked slightly, despite his attempt to keep it steady.

Clair smiled softly. "I know so."

Mark couldn't respond; he simply leaned forward, resting his elbows on the table, emotions swirling like the snow drifting outside.

"Mark, all I ask is that you leave yourself open—to love, to healing. You're a great dad, a wonderful teacher, but you're also a human being who needs a life outside those things as well. And maybe this is your time." Clair's eyes, twinkling with loving understanding, seemed to hold all the wisdom and tenderness a person could need. "Just give yourself the option to explore what could be."

Mark couldn't argue with her. His heart felt a stir of something long dormant, something he'd buried under the weight of grief and raising

Olivia on his own. But now, with Clair's words echoing gently in his mind, there was a glimmer of hope—one he hadn't thought possible before.

Chapter 6

Dawn painted the winter sky in gentle strokes of pink and gold as Emma stood before Laurel Ridge Elementary, her heart drumming a nervous rhythm against her ribs. The red brick facade rose before her like an old friend waiting to be reacquainted, its windows gleaming in the early morning light. Around her, the symphony of a school day beginning rose into the crisp December air—children's laughter carried in the wind, and the soft crunch of snow beneath tiny boots creating nature's own percussion.

A little girl in a purple coat sprinted past, her blonde pigtails bouncing beneath a knitted cap, and Emma couldn't help but smile. How many times had she run through these same doors as a child, full of dreams and wonder? Now here she was, thirty-five years old, starting fresh with dreams of a different kind.

She adjusted her wool scarf against the winter chill, her breath forming delicate clouds that danced upward like silent prayers. The familiar "You've got this" mantra echoed in her mind, but it felt different now—less like the confident assertion of her early nursing days and more like a gentle hope she was trying to nurture back to life.

Lord, she prayed silently, closing her eyes against the dazzle of sunlight on snow. *I know You brought me here for a reason. Help me see it clearly. Help me be the person these children need.*

Glancing at the building's familiar yet imposing structure, she clearly recognized she had first-day jitters. As a former hospital nurse, she was no stranger to nerves. But this—this new chapter—felt different. Raw, somehow. Like the old Emma, fresh out of nursing school, eager and filled with a sense of purpose... except now her confidence had been dented by all she had been through since then: loss, grief, the feeling of not knowing where she belonged. At thirty-five, this first day had a different weight than it had at twenty-two.

A burst of laughter drew her attention to where a young mother was kneeling in the snow, straightening her son's crooked backpack while he bounced impatiently from foot to foot.

Emma smiled and turned to walk up the school steps. She pulled open the heavy front door and stepped into the inviting atmosphere of Laurel Ridge Elementary School.

Immediately, she was enveloped by the unmistakable, reassuring scents of elementary school—a comforting blend of freshly sharpened pencils, craft glue, and the unforgettable scent of crayons. The smells, so distinct yet familiar, tugged at a deep-seated nostalgia. She couldn't help but chuckle softly to herself, feeling the memories stir as the hominess of it all seeped in.

The hallway hummed with life and possibility. Youthful voices echoed off walls decorated with bright artwork and encouraging words, their excitement infectious. The squeak of tennis shoes against polished floors created an impromptu rhythm section for the morning's symphony of activity. Someone's backpack had spilled open, sending crayons skittering across the floor like colorful shooting stars, while helpful hands scrambled to gather them up amidst giggles and cheerful chaos.

This wasn't the sterile halls of a hospital, where every moment could mean life or death. This was a place where small hurts could be soothed with cartoon bandages and gentle words, where a cup of ginger ale and a quiet moment could work miracles, where she could take the time to get to know the child behind the tiny injury or ailment they might have during a school day.

The first morning bell rang out suddenly, its clear tone reverberating through the building like a herald announcing the start of a new adventure. Children scurried to their classrooms, their energy leaving trails of joy in their wake.

Emma couldn't help the soft laugh that escaped her lips as memories washed over her like gentle waves. She could almost see her younger self—pigtails flying, knee socks slightly crooked—racing down these same halls with Wendy and Leah, their dreams as boundless as the blue sky beyond the classroom windows. These walls had seen countless stories: first crushes and scraped knees, triumphant spelling tests and playground victories, each one adding to the rich tapestry of childhood that seemed woven into the very bricks themselves.

After the sterile efficiency of hospital corridors, there was something beautifully chaotic about a place where construction paper hearts decorated bulletin boards and children's artwork transformed ordinary walls into galleries of imagination.

"Emma Whitman, right?" A warm voice threaded through the cacophony of morning activity.

Emma turned to find herself face-to-face with Sophia Grayson. She'd only spoken with the principal over the phone during her interview, but she recognized her voice right away. The woman's presence was exactly what Emma had imagined—and somehow more. Sophia carried herself with the kind of gentle authority that didn't need to announce itself. Her silver-streaked hair was carefully styled in an elegant shoulder-length hairstyle. Her friendly eyes sparkled with both wisdom and warmth.

"Welcome to Laurel Ridge Elementary!" Sophia's smile crinkled the corners of her eyes as she extended her hand. "I'm so glad to finally meet you in person."

Emma shook her offered hand, noting the firm but gentle grip. "Thank you for taking a chance on me," she replied, meaning every word. "It means a lot to be back here... though I have to admit, it feels very different from this side of things."

"Oh, I imagine it does," Sophia laughed, the sound rich and knowing. "I still remember my first day teaching years ago. I kept expecting someone to tell me I needed a hall pass!" She gestured down the corridor with an elegant wave. "Come on, let's get you settled in. The nurse's office has had quite the makeover since your student days, though I'm afraid the collection of plastic ice packs is still just as colorful."

The hallways of the school were alive with activity—a kindergartner zoomed past with his jacket half-on, a teacher called out cheerful good mornings, and somewhere nearby a door closed with a soft click. The symphony of school life played on, its familiar melody both comforting and exciting.

Her first-day nerves swirled thickly, though she wore a practiced calmness like armor. She'd been a nurse long enough to face bigger stresses than this, but today was different—less clinical, more personal. The fresh start she longed for was now unfolding.

With each step down the familiar-yet-strange hallway, her mind swayed between hope and hesitation like a pendulum. The antiseptic world of hospital rounds had become her comfort zone, but God was calling her to something different now—something that required her to be more than just Nurse Whitman. Here, she would need to be a comforter, a listener, a steady presence for little ones facing their own giants, whether those were playground scrapes or first-day jitters that mirrored her own.

"Here we are!" Sophia's voice carried a note of pride as she pushed open the door to the nurse's office. "Your new office."

Emma stepped into the space that would become her sanctuary for bandaged knees and worried hearts. The room was modest but welcoming—a sturdy desk waited patiently for its new keeper, its surface neat and ready with stacks of pristine forms. Two comfortable chairs stood sentinel nearby, positioned perfectly for concerned parent conferences or quiet conversations with teachers. The familiar scent of disinfectant hung lightly in the air, just enough to whisper "medical office" without shouting it.

Cheerful posters dotted the walls, their messages both practical and encouraging. "Wash Your Hands Thoroughly!" competed for attention with "Eat Healthy Foods for a Healthy Body" — brought a touch of familiarity, a nod to the world of pediatric care.

In the far corner, something caught Emma's eye—her very own coffee pot perched on a small table. She let out an appreciative sigh. All those early mornings and long afternoons would go down easier with a freshly brewed cup nearby.

Yet, the room was missing something. A bit spartan, she thought, walking further into the space. She pictured a few holiday decorations—perhaps a wreath or twinkle lights strung along the windowsill.

It wouldn't take much to make this a comforting room for worried or scared little ones that would visit her during the school day.

She could already picture herself here, tending to bumps and bruises, soothing small anxieties with gentle words and a smile. This would be her little haven, here at Laurel Ridge Elementary—a space of healing in more ways than one.

"This is perfect," Emma said, nodding.

"I'm glad you think so!" Sophia said brightly. "If you need anything—supplies, help, moral support, someone to explain the difference between playground drama and actual emergencies—you let me know."

Emma laughed, already feeling some of her nerves dissipate. "I appreciate that."

"Take some time to get settled," Sophia said, moving toward the door. "My office is just around the corner, a few doors down. Why don't you join me there in about fifteen minutes? We can chat about what to expect during a typical day—though I use the word 'typical' very loosely in elementary school!" She winked. "Any day might include anything from loose teeth to upset tummies."

Emma nodded, appreciating the kindness radiating from the principal's every word.

Once Sophia left, Emma set to work, placing her few personal effects on the desk.

***

Emma hadn't even fully turned the corner into the hallway after leaving Sophia's office when the collision happened.

One second, she was focusing on sorting through the day, and the next—books, folders, and papers were sent scattering onto the polished school floor. Instinctively, Emma bent down, muttering apologies, her cheeks flushing.

"Oh no, I'm so sorry!" she stammered as she reached for the scattered items.

"No, no—my fault entirely. I wasn't paying attention either..."

The voice froze her in place. Seventeen years melted away in an instant.

Emma's gaze traveled upward slowly, taking in the blue sweater, and the broad shoulders, until she met those warm brown eyes she'd tried so hard to forget. Mark Thompson stood before her, looking both the same and entirely different—time had left its gentle marks, but his eyes still held that same gentle intensity that had once made her feel like she was his entire world.

Mark Thompson.

Memories came rushing back like a dam breaking open. She blinked, nearly dropping the textbook again, unsure if this moment was real or some ghost she had accidentally conjured from the past.

"Mark?" she breathed out before she could stop herself.

His eyes—those soft, warm brown eyes she'd never forgotten—locked on hers as a wave of recognition swept across his face. For a moment, the world tilted, and it was just the two of them standing in a hallway similar to this when they were teenagers, sharing memories and laughter.

But now? Now, there was something almost impenetrable between them. Time. Wounds. Lives that had diverged. And hurt... from endings that were never fully explained.

Mark cleared his throat and shook his head, breaking the stillness. "Emma. I—uh—wow, this is... a surprise."

Emma nodded, trying to seem nonchalant despite the thudding pulse that raced through her. "Y-yeah. I, uh," she floundered, still gripping the textbook limply in her hand, her fingers feeling oddly numb. "I'm... the new school nurse."

Her voice fell away slightly, and she bit her lip.

The awkwardness thickened between them, only broken by the chaos surrounding them—children scurrying to class, distant laughter, shoes squeaking on floors.

Mark shifted and ran a hand through his hair, shaking off the initial shock. "I heard you moved back to Laurel Ridge."

"Just a few days ago, actually," Emma replied. "Andrew mentioned you were teaching here," she added.

Mark nodded. "Fourth grade. It's been a... a good fit. Olivia loves it here."

"Olivia?" she asked quietly, struggling to find normalcy in the conversation.

"Oh, I'm sorry. Olivia is my daughter. She's in the second grade." Mark's voice held just enough fondness to shift the tension between them slightly. "Hard to believe how fast she's growing up."

There it was—the softness she had always loved about Mark. The way he spoke of his daughter, the disarming gentleness that made even the sharp edges of her memories ease.

"I bet she's wonderful," Emma said, allowing herself a small smile despite the storm of emotions churning beneath the surface.

"She... she really is." Mark glanced down the hall, then back at Emma. For a few brief moments, they exchanged a look that carried the weight of years—of unspoken words and choices made long ago.

"I'm glad you're back." Mark said out of nowhere, almost surprising himself with how quickly the words tumbled from his lips. "I mean... I bet you're happy to be back home."

Heat crept up Emma's neck, and she instinctively glanced down at the books she was still holding. Biting her lip, she nodded in response.

For a beat, neither knew what to say next.

A small child rushed by them, bursting into one of the classrooms with pure first-grade exuberance, wholly unaware of the emotional whirlpool between Emma and Mark.

"It's... it's good to see you," Emma finally managed, though her voice trembled just slightly. She shifted the books in her arms as if they were a shield, bracing herself for the tidal wave of emotions that threatened to rise.

Mark hesitated, his brows furrowed in thought. He opened his mouth, but whatever words he sought seemed lost in the noise of the bustling hallway. Instead, he gave her a small, almost melancholic smile, one that hinted at things left unsaid for far too long.

"Yeah... you too," he said.

"Well, I'd better... I mean..." Emma stammered, gesturing awkwardly toward her office, desperate to break free of the charged atmosphere.

Mark, too, straightened slightly, nodding as if giving her the out she sought. "Yeah, sure," he said, stepping aside to let her pass. "We'll... we'll catch up sometime."

"Catch up?" She said, with a touch of attitude in her voice, as she handed his books to him.

Before he could respond, Emma hurried off toward her office, her heart still pounding in her chest, her mind racing with the myriad of what-ifs and bittersweet memories.

She didn't stop until she reached the safety of her little haven. She closed the door, leaned her back against it, and let out a shaky breath.

Chapter 7

Mark Thompson.

His name alone still had the power to unearth things she'd thought she had buried deep beneath the rubble of her adult life—uncomfortable truths about the girl she used to be and how part of that naïve young woman would never stop yearning for something she had long convinced herself was better left in the past.

For a moment, she pressed her hand to her chest, feeling the steady thrum of her heartbeat slow. *You can handle this*, she reminded herself. A whispered prayer danced on her lips again as she stood there, cocooned by the familiar air of antiseptic and winter's chill sneaking through the window seams.

"Lord, give me strength. Open my heart where it needs to be and please... make this feel manageable."

Emma took a deep breath, pushing herself off the door and moving toward her desk. There were children who would need her. Staff she had to introduce herself to. Maybe, just maybe, she could stay focused on that—for now. But even as she busied herself arranging supplies, the echo of Mark's presence lingered like the ringing of a school bell—a reminder that some paths, no matter how diverged, had a way of crossing again.

Her mind whirled as she sat behind her desk, shuffling papers just for something to do, anything to ground herself after the unexpected encounter with Mark. She had thought coming back home would be the start of something new. But sitting here now, after seeing Mark, she realized nothing could truly prepare you to face pieces of the past lingering like half-opened doors.

Memories of Mark flooded Emma's mind in a rush of vivid flashes: high school dances where they'd laughed and twirled beneath twinkling lights, lazy afternoons spent whitewater rafting on the New River, and cozy bonfire nights after football games, holding hands, every moment charged with unspoken possibility. All of it surged back into her consciousness with startling intensity, like the past had suddenly come too close to remain distant any longer.

Emma thought about one particular winter during her senior year of high school, back when she and Mark lived the carefree lives of two young people. She remembered how they'd both signed up to work the town's Christmas tree sale fundraiser—an idea Emma had thought would be simple and fun. But that day, sitting side by side at the registration table with snow gently falling around them, something had shifted between them, something deeper than the laughter and playful teasing they were used to. It was subtle, almost unspoken, yet there was an unshakable sense of closeness—like they belonged to each other in ways neither of them understood at the time.

She remembered watching Mark out there in the cold, bundled up in a navy jacket, the tips of his ears turning red as he helped families heft their trees into the back of pickup trucks. He would look back at her, their eyes would meet briefly, and her heart would stumble over itself each time, a rhythm of realization slowly unraveling within her. She had fallen completely in love.

Now—decades later, sitting alone in her quiet, sterile office—those old feelings pulled gently at the corners of her heart like a forgotten melody. But Emma knew better. Time had moved on. And they weren't the same two wide-eyed teenagers from years ago anymore.

Mark had loved and lost, just like her. They both carried ghosts of different heartaches, woven into the fabric of who they were now. The weight of grief had settled in both of their lives, carving out spaces no one else could touch.

The thought was sobering, but also strangely comforting. In a way, they were walking the same path now, both of them navigating the grief of moving forward after love had been torn away by tragedy.

Emma knew that Mark had lost his wife a few years ago. She could still recall the phone call from her mother, gently informing her of the tragedy, the tone of her voice soft with concern. At the time, Emma had been caught up in her own life in Pittsburgh—her demanding hospital shifts consuming her days. She had just started dating Rhett. When her mother shared the news about Mark, there had been a pang of sadness, a moment where time seemed to still and tug her heart back to Laurel Ridge for just a beat.

Mark had been a widower now for nearly four years, raising his daughter Olivia alone. A thin thread of guilt wound its way through her as she remembered hearing the news, and just how little she had done about it at the time. She should have at least called to extend her condolences, but she never had. She had felt awful when she found out, of course—her heart had genuinely hurt for him—but life, as it often did, kept moving. And so had she.

She shook her head and focused on the files in front of her. This wasn't a time for daydreams or questions about what might've been. She had a career to focus on—a life to rebuild one step at a time.

Just as she began arranging her paperwork with more determination, trying to steady herself against the echoes of the past, there was a soft knock at the door.

"Come in," she called, adjusting her posture and summoning a smile, even though her thoughts were anything but collected.

The door opened slightly, and a small, hesitant face peeked around the corner. A little girl with brown curls and curious brown eyes. She noticed the deep, soulful color of her eyes and the delicate features of her face, and immediately noticed the familiarity.

Unreal... God, you are really testing me today, aren't you?

"Hi. My teacher said I could come see you because I bumped my hand at recess." Her voice was soft and a bit shy.

Emma's heart skipped, tumbling gracelessly into her stomach. But her smile softened all the more as she met the girl's gaze. "Hello, my name's Emma, and I'm the new school nurse. What's your name?"

"Olivia."

Mark's daughter.

"Well, come on in, Olivia," Emma said, keeping her voice gentle and bright. "Let's take a look at that hand."

Olivia stepped in, clutching her right hand carefully to her chest. Her small frame seemed even tinier against the vastness of the office, her winter boots clomping softly on the floor as she approached the desk. Emma gestured toward the padded cot near the window, and with tentative steps, the girl hopped up, her feet swinging gently above the ground.

As Olivia stretched out her hand, Emma inspected it with a clinical yet caring eye. A slight bruise was forming just by the base of her thumb—nothing serious, but still enough to call for a little care and gentle concern.

Emma smiled, reaching for an ice pack from the small freezer she'd stocked earlier that morning. "This might feel a little cold at first, but it'll help with the bruise," she said, handing the pack over to Olivia, who took it with a brave little nod.

As Olivia pressed the ice to her hand, her wide eyes searched Emma's face, observing her with more intensity than most adults ever do.

"How are you liking second grade? I remember my elementary school days—those were full of busy, fun times," she said with a soft smile.

Olivia gave a small shrug, glancing down at her hand nervously. "I like it. Mrs. Davis is nice... and Daddy helps me with my homework because it's hard sometimes. I like gym class and story time the most." Her voice softened as she mentioned her father, and Emma immediately noticed the gleam in her eyes when she did.

Mark. Memories of him swept over Emma again, but she pushed them down, choosing to focus entirely on his little girl in front of her—the innocent warmth Olivia radiated, and the trust she seemed to naturally extend.

"Well, sounds like you've got it all figured out," Emma said, nodding toward the ice pack. "And this will make that little bump go away in no time."

"Do you know my daddy?" Olivia asked, her young eyes sharp and curious.

Emma's breath faltered for just a second, but she quickly recovered, offering a gentle smile. "Yes, I do," she said, her heart tugging unexpectedly. "A long time ago, when we were both younger. We went to school together."

Olivia's gaze never faltered, her expression a perfect mixture of wonder and intrigue. "Daddy tells stories sometimes about when he went to school. He's good at stories." She leaned in, her voice dropping to an almost secretive tone. "Were you friends with my daddy when you went to school with him?"

"Well," she said, mustering a soft laugh, "we knew each other, that's for sure. I guess you could say that yes, we were friends."

Olivia's smile grew satisfied with that answer for now.

A small knock on the door interrupted them. Both Emma and Olivia turned to see Sophia entering the office, one brow raised in amusement.

"I see someone found her way here already." Sophia grinned at Olivia. "Feeling better, sweetheart?"

Olivia nodded energetically. "Yep! Much better."

"Good," Sophia replied, nodding toward Emma before returning her attention to Olivia. "Let's get you back to class. I bet Mrs. Davis is wondering how you are."

Olivia hopped off the cot, leaving the ice pack behind, and gave a quick wave to Emma before hurrying toward the door.

"Bye, Miss Emma!" Olivia called over her shoulder as she disappeared.

Emma stood by her desk, her thoughts racing far faster than her heart could keep up with. That child—so sweet, so full of life—was a piece of Mark, a living, breathing extension of the person she used to know so well.

Emma sighed softly, brushing back a lock of hair from her face.

The bell rang in the distance, signaling the start of the lunch hour, pulling her back to reality. She sat and leaned her elbows on the desk, glancing out the window at the snow just beginning to fall again.

Her life, like the snowfall, was slowly shifting.

Chapter 8

The scent of roast beef drifted from the oven and filled the parsonage's cozy kitchen as Emma set the silverware down on the table. Andrew stood by the stove, stirring gravy with the ease of someone who was used to fending for himself.

"Okay, so give it to me straight," Andrew said, lifting the spoon to taste the gravy. "You just happened to bump into him? I mean, come on."

Emma rolled her eyes, adjusting the last fork on the table. "Andrew, do you seriously think I planned it? Trust me, if I was orchestrating a reunion, it definitely wouldn't have been scattering a fourth grader's teacher's books and student assignments across the floor."

Andrew chuckled, wiping his hands on a dish towel as he turned to face her. "Maybe not your best moment, but still," he continued with a teasing smirk, "That's... something, huh? You sure it's not a sign?"

Emma paused for half a second, then quickly resumed folding the napkins, determined not to let him see the flicker of uncertainty that had settled in the back of her mind. "A sign? That's a stretch, even for you—unless the sign is to be more careful where I'm walking."

"Oh, come on. You never know, Em," Andrew said, crossing his arms and leaning casually against the counter. "Life's funny that way. He was your high school sweetheart, after all."

She shot him a pointed look, though her lips tugged into a reluctant smile. "That was a lifetime ago. You know, when we still thought the height of excitement was sneaking ice cream out of the church freezer at the Christmas play rehearsals."

Andrew grinned, eyes twinkling at the old memory. "Now, that was a rush for any teenager."

Emma rolled her eyes, leaning against the back of her chair. "Mark and I were kids. That's ancient history. Besides, there's no way anything would happen now. He's got a daughter... and there's so much..."

"History?" Andrew finished, his voice softening just a little with understanding.

She nodded, crossing her arms over her chest, her pulse quickening as she tried to shrug off the warmth she felt at the mention of Mark's daughter, Olivia—the sweet little girl who'd shown up in her office with bright, curious eyes. "And no offense, but I didn't move back to Laurel Ridge for a 'second-chance romance.' I came here to heal, to figure out my life... you know... start something new."

Andrew tipped his head sympathetically, but the teasing tone lingered in his voice. "Sure. Just don't forget that healing doesn't have an expiration date. And," he wagged a finger at her, "life has a funny way of reconnecting people just when they least expect it. Ask me how I know."

A light ping of curiosity flickered. "Does this wisdom have something to do with anyone I know?"

"Take Mom and Dad, for example—they dated in high school, went their separate ways, and ended up at different colleges in different states. Then life happened, and they reunited after they both graduated from college. And look at us all now, all these years later, they are happily married and raised three fine kids. You just never know where your path might take you. I'm telling you, God has a way of working things out in ways we don't always expect. So, maybe bumping into Mark wasn't just a coincidence after all," he said.

Emma scoffed, though not without a small smile. "That sounds like a line straight out of a holiday rom-com on television. You've been watching too many Christmas specials."

Andrew leaned over, eyes glinting. "Hey, I don't mind being the funny, best brother in the world character in your own real life movie romance, as long as I get top billing."

Emma shook her head and laughed as she turned her attention back to the dinner table. She loved her brother, and his playfulness was often exactly what she needed. But she refused to entertain this notion. Falling for Mark again wasn't in the cards. "Okay, well, for the record," she said as she grabbed the gravy and set it on the table, "I'm not looking to bring any old love interest into the picture. I'm doing fine just dealing with life right now as it is."

"Sure," Andrew replied, turning serious for a brief moment. "But if you ask me, finding love again doesn't mean you're not allowed to still process Rhett's death. Grief and healing don't follow a straight line. You can heal from one heartbreak while letting your heart open to something else."

Emma sighed, taking a deep breath before responding. "I'm not ready for that."

Before Andrew could respond, the timer on the oven beeped, and he moved effortlessly to pull the roast from the oven. Emma smiled in appreciation of the distraction, her mind swirling faster than she could comprehend.

They sat down at the table, but her thoughts stirred inside her like a whirlwind. Rekindling old flames? No way. She wasn't ready for that. Didn't want it, either. Her focus was on finding peace, not complicating her life with unexpected feelings for a man from her past who had walked away from her as if he had never cared. Emma convinced herself that she could let it go. That seeing Mark again didn't mean anything.

She joined hands with Andrew, as he thanked God for their meal, their family, and the blessing of being together again. His words were simple and comforting, grounding in a way that centered her soul just a little.

"And Lord," Andrew closed, a grin in his prayerful tone, "thank you for bringing Emma back, even though she tries way too hard to ignore the obvious blessings in front of her... like maybe the occasional friendly face from the past."

Emma squeezed Andrew's hand—hard—earning herself a chuckle as they said a mutual "Amen."

Yeah, she thought. *Friends. Just friends.*

***

Later that evening, after the dishes were washed, and the house had fallen quiet, Emma stood in her room. The sounds of the night bled through the windows—the wind stirring through the trees, the occasional jingle of the wind chimes Andrew had hung outside.

She sank onto the bed, still staring out the window as her thoughts wandered.

Seeing Mark had thrown her off balance. Not in a bad way, necessarily—just in a way that made her question things she wasn't ready to question.

Emma knelt beside her bed, feeling the soft ache of restrained tears washing over her as she clasped her hands in front of her.

"Lord," she whispered, "I came here thinking I'd find peace. I thought healing meant moving on from everything—Rhett, my old life in Pittsburgh. I never thought coming back would stir up so many unanswered questions. Seeing Mark again—it brought up parts of my heart that, I thought, were buried. Buried deep."

Her voice wavered slightly as she closed her eyes tighter. "I don't know what to do, Lord. Help me understand what You want for me. If it's to forgive... to open my heart again... or to just let go, I need Your clarity. And if I'm meant to love again, give me the courage I need to trust You completely."

Chapter 9

Mark opened the front door, letting in a swirl of cold air as his boots thudded on the hardwood floor. Beside him, Olivia hopped inside, shaking the snow from her hair and giggling as she hurried to unlace her boots. From the direction of the kitchen came the soft hum of Clair's singing, mingled with the rich, comforting aroma of vegetable stew simmering on the stove.

Mark shrugged off his coat, giving it a quick dust to shake off the remaining flakes before hanging it by the door. Olivia was already halfway out of her coat and boots, her fingers fumbling with excitement. The moment her feet were free, she darted off toward the kitchen before he could even say a word.

"Grandma!" she called, her little voice echoing through the house with a mixture of joy and anticipation.

Mark shook his head and smiled.

"There's one of my favorite grandsons," Eli said with a chuckle from the living room, his voice raspy with age but still filled with the warmth of humor that made Mark smile every time. "Hope you're ready to get your hands dirty, kid."

Mark grinned, his muscles already relaxing a bit from the chilly walk over. "Don't worry, Pops. I've wrestled with enough plumbing issues of my own in the past. Fixing your kitchen sink should be a breeze."

Eli laughed from his recliner, waving off Mark's remark. "You've softened up over the years, son. Teaching fourth graders is one thing. Wrestling my kitchen sink? Another story."

Mark knelt down beside the sink, grabbing the toolbox Eli had already pulled from the closet, and began fiddling with the pipe. It wasn't anything too serious—just a bit of wear and tear—but the chance to stay busy did wonders for Mark's restless thoughts.

After a few minutes of banter between Mark and his grandfather about the Winter Festival preparations and Olivia's excitement for the church Christmas play, Eli's voice dropped to a quieter tone.

"Anything interesting happen today at work?"

Mark paused mid-tightening and glanced sideways at his grandfather, who watched him with that knowing look he'd long mastered—one that could make a man confess his deepest secrets without saying a word.

Mark sighed, refocusing on the pipe. "Yeah... I ran into Emma today."

Eli hummed, a soft sound of appreciation that held more power than it should have. "Emma Whitman. Now that's a name I've not heard in quite some time. How was that?"

Mark set the wrench aside, leaning back on his heels as he brushed his hands together to get rid of the dust. "It was... surprising. I didn't expect to see her so soon, but really, it was inevitable with her working at the school now."

"She's the new nurse, right?" Eli asked, though it was more of a statement.

"Yeah." Mark's voice sounded distant, even to himself.

Eli leaned forward in his chair slightly, watching his grandson carefully. "How do you feel about that?"

Mark stood, adjusting his flannel shirt before sitting in the chair opposite Eli. "It's... complicated."

"As most things worth anything usually are," Eli replied softly, his eyes crinkling at the corners with understated wisdom.

Mark couldn't help but chuckle. "It's not like that, Pops. I'm not thinking about anything like... romance or whatever. It would be ridiculous. My focus is on Olivia, and honestly, she's my whole world. Bringing something—or someone—into her life would be... unfair. Plus, I've got enough to worry about with the festival, the play, and work." He waved a hand dismissively, trying to sound sure of his reasoning.

But Eli saw right through him, as always.

"You sure about that? You and Emma had a really strong relationship at one point?" Eli asked, straightforward but not unkind.

Mark found it challenging whenever his grandfather asked these deep questions—the kind that cut right to the core. The truth was, seeing Emma today had rattled him more than he cared to admit. But how could he even consider the possibility of diving into something—anything—while raising his daughter on his own? Maggie's memory was still there, as present as ever, and opening that chapter of vulnerability felt like a tangle of emotions and confusion he wasn't prepared for.

Eli leaned back as a smile edged its way onto his lips. "You know, Mark, the Lord works in ways we don't fully understand most of the time. A reunion like that? Might seem like a reminder that there's still more in this life yet to be written for the both of you."

Mark shook his head quickly, the scoff escaping before he could stop it. "Don't start planning wedding bells, Pops. There's no way Emma and I... not after everything."

Eli didn't push—he never did. Instead, he simply said, "We often stand in the way of our own faith when we're too afraid to look beyond the grief. Sometimes all the Lord asks of us is to keep our hearts open enough to hear what He has planned."

Mark's chest ached at his grandfather's words, but he didn't respond. Instead, he stood, moving toward the door with a half-hearted grin. "Thanks, Grandpa. I'll see about that open heart stuff, but right now... well, I think I've done all the emotional wrenching I can handle for one day."

Eli's eyes twinkled with humor. "Just fixin' the pipes for now, then?"

"Exactly."

***

Mark sat at his dining room table, a stack of math assignments spread before him, but his thoughts kept drifting back to his unexpected encounter with Emma. The more he thought about it, the more amusing and almost cliché it seemed—the kind of moment that might play out in a cheesy holiday movie. Of course, he would run into his old flame on her very first day working at the same school. Life had a strange way of throwing curveballs when you least expected them. He shook his head with a quiet chuckle, realizing just how much the day had surprised him. Life sure did have its sense of humor.

He couldn't help but wonder why, after all these years, she had come back to Laurel Ridge. From what he had heard, her life in Pittsburgh seemed settled—successful, even. Word had spread around town that Emma had risen to head nurse at one of the city's leading hospitals, a position she had worked hard to achieve, he was sure. So why return now?

Mark stared at his cell phone in the quiet stillness of the house. Olivia was tucked into bed, sleeping soundly. He picked up the phone, his thumb hovering over the screen for a moment before he tapped Andrew's name.

Andrew and Mark had been best friends since elementary school. And considering the close bond they shared, coupled with Andrew being Emma's brother, Mark knew he could count on him to be straightforward. When it came to Emma's return, Mark needed the truth—without the usual dodging or careful wording. He dialed Andrew's number, and on the third ring, a familiar voice picked up.

"Hey, man. What's up?" Andrew's voice carried the easy familiarity of years of friendship. It wasn't just casual chit-chat. It was Andrew's way of saying, "I'm here, and I already know this is about more than the weather."

"Hey," Mark replied, leaning back in his chair as he tried to find the right words. "I, uh, ran into Emma today. At the school."

There was a brief pause on the other end of the line—a pause that hung in the air like the calm before a playful storm.

"Yeah, so I heard," Andrew finally said, his voice laced with a knowing grin Mark could practically hear over the phone. "And how did that go?"

Mark let out a soft laugh, rubbing the back of his neck. "It was... surprising... It startled me, actually. I didn't know she was starting today," he muttered, trailing off as memories of their brief interaction flooded his mind once more.

Andrew chuckled. "Yeah, well, that's how bumps in the hallway tend to go. You okay?"

"Yeah, yeah. It just caught me off guard, you know? It's been years, and seeing her again...," Mark said, his voice quiet, laced with the weight of unresolved feelings.

Another brief pause, this one more thoughtful.

"Look, I get it," Andrew replied after a beat. "You and Emma had something special back then. And seeing her again is bound to bring up old memories."

"What's Emma's story?" Mark asked. "Why'd she come back to town? She didn't really say much when I saw her, but I could sense there's more going on."

Andrew sighed quietly, the kind of sigh that told Mark he wasn't going to get the full rundown without some emotional context. "Emma's been through a lot over the last year. You know she lost her fiancé, Rhett, right? The car accident?"

Mark's breath caught.

"I had no idea," Mark said.

"Yeah, it's been rough for her," Andrew replied, his voice full of empathy. "That's one of the reasons she's here. She needed a change—needed to come home to figure things out. She wants to start a new life here."

Mark took a breath. "I see," he murmured, his fingers tracing the wooden grains on his dining room table.

"I had no idea she'd gone through something like that," Mark said, his voice heavy with regret.

"It was a really rough time," Andrew said, his voice low. "She was in the car with him when the accident happened. Spent a few days in the hospital herself. After that, everything just... collapsed for her. She's doing better than she was, but she's still not the old Emma. Not completely, anyway."

Mark stayed quiet, absorbing the weight of Andrew's words.

"When your grandmother decided to retire from the school, Mom mentioned it to Emma—let her know the nurse position would be opening up," Andrew continued. "It didn't take her long to think about it. Just a few days, really. Then she applied, and before you knew it, she had the job. No problems there. Packed up her whole life in Pittsburgh and left it all behind within a matter of weeks."

"Wow," Mark said.

"Yeah," Andrew continued, a note of reflective thought in his voice. "Honestly, her decision to pack it all up and return home took me by surprise. I mean, I'm glad she's here, don't get me wrong—but I never imagined Emma would leave Pennsylvania. She really loved her life there... until, well, everything came crashing down around her."

"I feel for her," Mark said, his voice soft with understanding. "I know all too well what that's like to lose someone you love."

Andrew's voice softened with understanding on the other end of the line. "Yeah, I know you do." There was a pause, a natural rhythm of connection borne from their years of friendship. "That's why, of all people, you're probably one of the few who can really get where she's coming from. Losing someone like that... it leaves a mark you never fully shake."

Mark sighed, rubbing the bridge of his nose. "It's difficult. The pain, the healing... it's messy."

"I get it, really." Andrew paused, his tone softening further. "You two were once close. Maybe now, more than anything, she just needs a friend. Someone who understands."

"I don't know, Andrew," Mark murmured, his voice weighted with uncertainty.

"Start slow," Andrew continued. "Be the friend who's walked that road."

Mark stared out the window into the snowy darkness. "I'm not sure if it's that simple."

Andrew, sensing the hesitance, chuckled softly. "Well, enough about the heavy stuff. How's Olivia?"

Mark's shoulders relaxed as a smile flickered at the mention of his daughter. "She's got more festive energy right now than a pack of elves. She reminds me daily we need to get a Christmas tree still."

"She's a good kid," Andrew said with a grin in his voice.

"Yeah," Mark said, his heart full at the thought of Olivia's boundless spirit. "She's my everything."

A beat of silence fell between them before Andrew spoke again. "Hey, just keep yourself open-ended, alright? That's all I'm saying. You're doing a great job with Olivia, but maybe—just maybe—there's room in your life to be a friend to Emma. I really think she needs as many people in her life right now as possible."

Mark's chest tightened, but he found himself nodding even though Andrew couldn't see him. "I'll keep that in mind."

"Well, you said it yourself—life's funny that way, right?" Andrew chuckled, then added, "Talk soon, man."

"Yeah, soon," Mark echoed, though his thoughts were tangled as the call ended.

He placed his phone down on the table, the quiet settling back into the house like a fresh dusting of snowfall. Outside, the wind whispered softly through the trees, while inside, everything was still save for the ticking of the kitchen clock and the occasional stir of the fireplace embers in the hearth.

Mark rubbed the back of his neck before resting his hands on the table. He stared at the stack of ungraded papers in front of him, but when he reached for the red pen to get back to work, his mind refused to cooperate. Instead of math problems, it was the image of Emma that filled his thoughts—her wide, surprised eyes when they'd bumped into each other; the air between them strained, like neither quite knew how to step forward.

His heart ached, but not just from nostalgia. It was something deeper, more tender, more cautious—like the edges of a scar long since healed, but still tender to the touch.

Mark exhaled slowly, pushing the stack of papers aside before leaning his elbows on the table. He ran his hands over his face, letting them linger there as the weight of the day settled in.

The familiar creaking of the floor upstairs broke his thoughts. He tilted his head toward the noise, smiling gently when he heard the soft shuffle of Olivia's feet.

"Daddy?" Olivia's voice was a drowsy whisper from the hallway; she peeked her head around the corner, her hair slightly messy and her eyes half-closed.

Mark smiled, standing up and crossing the room to meet her. "What are you doing up, Peanut?"

"I had a dream... about Mommy," Olivia whispered, rubbing her eyes with her small fists.

Mark knelt down beside her, the sudden shift from his thoughts about Emma to memories of Maggie feeling like a swift tug on his heart. He took Olivia's hands in his and gently pulled her into a hug. "You miss her, huh?"

Olivia nodded, her chin resting on his shoulder. "Do you think Mommy's watching over us, Daddy?"

Mark pressed his cheek against her hair, his arms gentle but firm around her. He closed his eyes for a moment, feeling the weight of both the question and the grief—so simple in the way Olivia asked and yet carrying the weight of everything unsaid.

"I think Mommy is always watching over us," he whispered softly. "And she's always right here with us, in our hearts."

Olivia sniffled slightly, then pulled back to look at him, her eyes wide and filled with a child's version of hope. "I had a dream she was singing to me like she used to... the song about the stars."

Mark felt his chest tighten but smiled through it, his voice warm. "That was one of her favorites."

Olivia leaned her head against his shoulder, still clutching his hand. "I miss her."

"I miss her too, Peanut." Mark whispered, pressing a kiss into her hair. "I always will."

Their shared silence stretched across the room, filled with soft, unspoken feelings that only grief and love could bring. After a few moments, Mark stood, lifting Olivia in his arms. "But you know what? You've got so many people here who love you—me, Grandpa Eli, Grandma Claire."

Olivia nodded sleepily, her small arms looping around his neck. "Yeah."

Mark carried her back upstairs, the weight of her small body feeling safe and familiar in the quiet night. As he placed her gently back into bed, tucking the quilt snugly around her shoulders, Olivia's eyes began to flutter shut once more.

"Night, Daddy," she whispered as she grabbed her stuffed bunny closer.

"Goodnight, Liv," Mark whispered back.

Chapter 10

A lively atmosphere filled the Laurel Ridge Community Church's recreation hall as townsfolk gathered to plan the church's Christmas play, their conversations blending with the sounds of coffee mugs clinking and shifting chairs. The room was filled with excitement, from the Christmas lights strung here and there around the room to the festive garlands draped along the windows. As she entered the hall, the joy of the occasion immediately eased Emma's anxieties while she scanned the crowd for friends.

It didn't take long before she spotted her brother, standing at the front of the room, a clipboard in hand as he greeted volunteers with his usual good-natured grin. To his right stood Leah and Wendy, chatting with Martha, her apron still tied around her waist, as if she'd shown up straight from work.

And there they were—Mark and Olivia—sitting near the back of the room. Olivia was perched on the edge of a chair, swinging her legs back and forth, while Mark sat beside her, leaning back in his seat with the casual posture of someone who had done this many times before. His presence brought a flurry of nerves.

Emma settled into a chair near the front, hoping the familiar buzz of conversation and laughter would calm the rising tide of emotions within her. The bustling energy of the room—warm and lively, filled with old friends and neighbors—should have been a comfort, but instead, it only heightened her sense of being unmoored, like a small boat adrift in a sea of nostalgia.

She straightened her posture and clasped her hands in her lap, forcing her focus onto the meeting at hand. There was work to be done, volunteer roles to be filled, and she needed to give her full attention to the moment. Yet, try as she might, her thoughts refused to fall in line, wandering instead to the swirling undercurrents of memories and feelings she'd been keeping at bay.

Her eyes swept the room, catching glimpses of people she'd known her whole life. They were all faces from a time when life was unblemished and simple, when her future had seemed so clear. And then—there was Mark.

Her heart felt both like it was in a free-fall, and yet tethered, held by invisible strands that connected her to that man who once filled every corner of her heart.

Stop it, Emma, she thought, blinking and looking away.

She inhaled deeply and exhaled, determined to push down the confusion, the tangled knot of emotions that churned whenever she saw him. Mark wasn't just her past—he was her reminder of what she had once wanted, but lost.

Leah, Wendy, and Martha settled next to Emma, taking the seats flanking her on either side. Leah gave her a soft nudge, a welcoming smile dancing on her lips, while Wendy whispered a quick greeting. Martha, whose apron strings were still loosely knotted around her waist, sat down with a small sigh of contentment, clearly glad to be off her feet, though the cheerful energy that surrounded her was unmistakable.

"I see you've been claimed for the volunteer party," Leah murmured playfully under her breath, glancing toward the front where Andrew stood, holding court with his usual friendly authority. "No escaping now."

Emma chuckled softly, the nervous edge she'd felt earlier lessening slightly in the comforting presence of her old friends.

Martha gently leaned over, patting Emma's arm with a warm, motherly touch. "I'm so glad to see you here, Emma."

Emma's heart squeezed at those simple words.

Smiling, Emma turned her gaze to Andrew as he began addressing the room. "Alright, everyone, let's go ahead and get started! First off, a big thank you to all the volunteers. As you know, the Christmas Play is one of our most cherished events the church puts on, and I'm so grateful you've all decided to pitch in to help make it a success."

Polite applause filled the room, and Andrew began outlining the different areas where volunteers were needed.

"As most of you know, the children's play is a heart and soul tradition here," Andrew smiled, glancing down at his paper. "Last year's production went off without a hitch, thanks to some of our more... gifted organizers."

There was a soft chuckle from the room, and Emma spotted Mark smiling to himself, clearly one of those repeat volunteers. From the corner of her eye, she watched as Olivia fidgeted excitedly beside him.

"This year," Andrew continued, "we'll need someone special to help coordinate the children's costumes. This involves not only making sure each child has what they need but also overseeing light sewing or alterations as needed, and—if you'll all pray for us—keeping the shepherds from running off with the wise men's gifts mid-play, as they did last year."

Laughter erupted across the room again.

Andrew scanned the crowd, his gaze landing directly on her. "Emma, do you think you could lend a hand with the costumes this year?"

Emma blinked. She was here to reconnect with the community, right? After a moment's hesitation, she smiled and nodded. "Sure, I'd love to help with the costumes."

Andrew beamed. "Great! And Mark has been helping with the play for years, so I'm sure you two will make a good team."

The words struck her like a soft jolt. Emma's eyes locked with Mark's for a brief second, and she saw the surprise in his expression—though it quickly softened into an agreeable nod. He raised his hand in a small wave, silently acknowledging the new partnership.

***

As the meeting broke out into smaller groups, Emma sat across from Mark at a long rectangular table, papers spread out between them with the details about the play and a list of necessary costumes. The initial awkwardness of their proximity hung in the air like frost on a windowpane—chilly and fragile.

Mark cleared his throat. "So, costumes... I guess we can start with the basic ones. Mary, Joseph, the wise men... though last year Liam's camel costume was way too big, so we should probably check the measurements this time before just... you know, winging it. The poor kid could barely walk."

Emma smirked, her voice laden with a playful edge. "Good advice. We wouldn't want a repeat of last year's runaway shepherd—just walking off in the middle of everything without so much as a word. That could really throw things off, don't you think?"

She threw a sidelong glance at Mark, her eyes gleaming with just enough mischief to make it clear she wasn't talking about the Christmas play anymore.

Mark's smile dimmed as he caught Emma's remark and what she was referencing. His fingers stilled on the papers spread before them, and his eyes flickered with a mix of emotion as if considering a reply but unsure how to wade into the waters she had just stirred.

"Yeah," he finally spoke, his voice quieter. "I suppose walking off never really solves anything." He offered a tight, apologetic smile, his gaze lingering over her face for a moment before dropping back to the papers.

There it was—acknowledgment, subtle but pointed enough to let her know she hadn't misfired. The past hung between them like a snow-covered branch, fragile and heavy, yet burdened with the knowledge that one wrong move could cause it to crack.

Martha, overhearing their conversation from the next table, piped in cheerfully, "You know, I'm still convinced we should give the wise men a bit more flair this year. Maybe a velvet cape or two—or perhaps a festive plaid skirt! It's high fashion in Scotland, after all." She winked mischievously.

Mark laughed, shaking his head at Martha's suggestion. "I'm not sure our wise men are ready for a fashion statement quite that bold, Martha."

Emma smiled at their banter, the tension in her chest easing a little. These small, familiar moments—the easy laughter, the warmth of old friendships—were reminders of why she had returned home in the first place. Yet, despite the comforting atmosphere, the prickling irritation she felt with Mark sitting so close was hard to ignore.

Get it together, Emma, she thought, taking a deep breath. You're here for the kids—not to stir up old emotions.

As they sifted through old notes for the Christmas play, the conversation between them began to flow more naturally, the initial awkwardness slowly ebbing away like a tide pulled back to sea. Mark thumbed through the stack of papers, crossing off costumes as they reviewed each one.

"So, about staffing," Mark said, bringing them back to the matter at hand. "We'll need some extra sets of hands for sewing alterations. Last time, I tried helping out with a needle, and let's just say it wasn't my finest moment."

Emma arched a brow, her smile softening into something fonder. "You? Sewing? I would've loved to see that."

He leaned back in his chair, his eyes sparking with amusement. "Trust me, you wouldn't. Let's just say I discovered my talents are better suited elsewhere."

The playful banter between them carried a familiar rhythm, each comment a buoy thrown into the water. But beneath it was the unspoken undercurrent, the sense that they both knew there was more unsaid—things that had nothing to do with costumes or stitching.

Mark's smile faltered just slightly, but enough for Emma to notice. His gaze dropped to the paper in front of him, pausing as if deciding whether to press forward or stay in the safe harbor of light conversation. He cleared his throat.

"Emma, I didn't... I mean, I wasn't expecting we'd be working together on this play," he said, his voice tinged with a hint of something—whether it was gratitude, surprise, or something else, Emma wasn't quite sure. "Not that it's a bad thing. It's good. Really."

A brief silence passed between them, the chatter of volunteers filling the space between thoughts. Emma's fingers traced the edge of the paper in front of her—a small, absent motion that mirrored the shift in the mood. The teasing tone had faded, giving way to something softer, more reflective.

"I didn't expect this either, you know. And whether or not this is a good situation... well, that's a matter of opinion," she said, her eyes still on the paper. "I'm not all that surprised Andrew arranged things this way. It's his clever way of nudging us back together."

Mark's gaze softened, his brows lifting just a touch, as if realizing what she wasn't saying aloud. "Well, then maybe this was meant to be," he said. His eyes held hers for a moment, an invitation of sorts—an opening left for her to explore if she wanted.

For a heartbeat, Emma considered delving in, letting the moment stretch out and breathe, but before she could respond, a little hand tugged on the sleeve of her sweater.

"Miss Emma?"

Emma turned, smiling warmly at the little girl. "Hi, Olivia."

"I remember you! You're the new nurse at school. You helped me when I bumped my hand."

Emma's smile broadened, her heart-softening instantly. "That's right! How's your hand now?"

"Good as new," Olivia chirped, showing Emma her hand proudly.

Mark watched the interaction closely, his expression softening into something tender and unreadable.

Olivia leaned closer, her curiosity getting the better of her as she noticed something about Emma. "Miss Emma, why do you have those funny lines on your neck?" Her finger brushed ever so gently over the light scar peeking out from underneath Emma's turtleneck.

Emma inhaled slightly. She hadn't expected Olivia's question, but of course, children noticed what adults tried to hide.

"I...," Emma hesitated before deciding it was better to be honest and simple. "I was in a car accident, sweetie," she said. "That's how I got these," she said as she ran a finger along the side of her neck.

Olivia's bright eyes widened with wonder. "Wow. Does it hurt?"

Emma chuckled. "Not anymore. I'm all better now."

The girl nodded sagely, then turned toward her father. "Daddy, did you know Miss Emma was in a car accident?"

Mark froze for a moment.

"I'm really sorry about Olivia's questions," Mark said softly, his voice threaded with quiet empathy. His gaze met Emma's, holding it for a moment longer than usual. "But I truly am sorry for everything you've been through."

Emma forced herself to hold his gaze, her heart pounding in her chest. The tenderness in his voice—the softness in his eyes—made her breath catch. He knew loss... he understood pain in a way only someone who has walked through it could.

"It's alright," Emma reassured, voice soft but steady. "Kids speak their minds—it's just how they see the world." There was more she might have said, much more left unsaid, simmering beneath the surface. But for now, that simple truth would have to be enough.

"Good thing you got better, Miss Emma! Now we can work on making my angel costume all sparkly!" Olivia said.

The gentle break in tension was a relief. Emma laughed, grateful for Olivia's ability to defuse a situation with charm and innocence.

"Absolutely," Emma agreed with a smile. "We'll make sure it's extra sparkly."

As the afternoon slipped into early evening, work on the play preparations continued. The lively sound of other volunteers filled the recreation hall as conversations flowed comfortably once more. Mark and Emma settled into an easier rhythm as they dug through totes of costumes, checking to be certain they were still in good condition, occasionally sharing glances, soft smiles, and warmer exchanges.

"So, how long has it been since you helped with a church play?" Mark asked, as he scribbled down notes.

"Oh, quite a while," Emma replied, tilting her head in thought. "High school, probably. It's a little surreal to be back, honestly. I attended a few churches while I lived in Pittsburgh, but none of them ever felt quite like home the way this one in Laurel Ridge does. The congregations there were so large, and it was challenging to really connect with anyone on a deeper level. Plus, with my hectic schedule, I never had much time to volunteer or get involved the way I can here."

Mark nodded, his expression thoughtful. "It must feel strange... leaving behind one life just to come back to another."

Emma's brow furrowed as she nodded. "Yeah. It's... it's complicated."

"Life usually is," Mark replied quietly, his gaze skimming over the list of costumes they still needed to find and check for the play. He hesitated, before adding, "Coming home can be hard. But... it's also a chance to start fresh, you know?"

Emma glanced over at Olivia, who was busy chatting animatedly with Leah and Wendy a few yards away, her joy contagious.

"Yeah. Coming home is about starting over again for me—about reconnecting with what matters most," Emma replied. "I was in a rut back in Pennsylvania. When mom called to tell me about the school nursing job opening, it didn't take me long to jump on the idea of coming home. It's one of the things in life that, I think, was meant to be."

Mark's expression softened, his gaze lingering on Emma a fraction longer than what felt comfortable. "I get that," he said, his voice gentle but sure. "It's strange, isn't it? Life has this way of circling you back to where you're supposed to be, even if the path there is... crooked. I never thought I'd end up raising Olivia on my own, but... here we are."

Emma nodded, feeling a wave of empathy sweep over her. The weight of their shared past losses—hers with Rhett, his with Maggie—hung between them like an invisible thread. Both had forged new lives from brokenness, though neither one could predict where that journey would fully lead them.

"You're doing a great job with Olivia, I can tell," Emma said, turning the conversation toward his daughter, who was now laughing with another little girl—Isabelle Foster—at a nearby table. "She's... really special. She's a sweet little girl. You must be proud."

Mark smiled, following her gaze to where Olivia and Isabelle worked together on stringing popcorn for a garland. His voice softened as he spoke, not taking his eyes off his daughter. "Yeah, I am. She's my whole world, you know? It's not always easy, but... I wouldn't trade it for anything."

Emma glanced down at her hands, her fingers running absently over the seam of a costume. There was something in Mark's simplicity—his matter-of-fact adoration for Olivia—that tugged at her. He wasn't trying to impress anyone. He wasn't pretending it was all easy. He was just... trying, doing his best, moment by moment. It made her wonder what it might be like to be a part of that world, to feel that unconditional love and belonging again.

Mark cleared his throat. "I know it's not simple, coming back here after everything you've been through. But it's good to see you again, Emma. Really."

Before Emma could respond, Olivia came bounding over with a garland of popcorn, her face lit with excitement. "Miss Emma! Look! Isabelle and I made this for the Christmas tree! Do you think it's long enough?"

Emma's eyes sparkled as she leaned down to admire the garland. "It's wonderful! I think it'll look perfect on the tree."

Olivia beamed at her. "Can you help us hang it?"

Emma nodded, rising to follow Olivia as she scampered back to the small group of children at the other end of the room near the Christmas tree that was waiting to be decorated. As she did, she felt Mark's gaze following her, the weight of unspoken things hanging lightly between them. They weren't kids anymore. And their paths had diverged so long ago. But here they were, both a little broken, yet trying to find warmth in the midst of winter days.

Chapter 11

The last of the voices murmured softly in the background as chairs scraped the floor and coats were pulled tight against the winter air inside the rec hall. The meeting was winding down, the satisfaction of a productive day visible on the faces of the volunteers. Emma hadn't realized how much she'd needed this—the rhythm of normal lives enjoying the company of one another, the gentle hum of a community banding together.

Andrew stood at the front of the room, flipping through his clipboard one last time. "Alright, I think that's everything for today, folks. Let's meet back here tomorrow after church, and we can start working on some of the finer details for the children's Christmas play."

Around her, Emma saw nods of agreement—including Mark's. He was sitting across from her, Olivia by his side, her little legs swinging off the chair as she giggled about something Wendy had said to her.

Emma suppressed the smile that tugged at her lips. She was supposed to be focusing on the task at hand—outlining their duties for tomorrow—but her thoughts couldn't seem to stay steady around

Mark. There was an ease in the way he sat, arms crossed casually, that unsettled her more than it should.

"We'll meet right after service, then?" Mark asked, his voice cutting through Emma's thoughts.

"I'll be here," Wendy chimed in. "Leah and I will continue going through the decorations for the play tomorrow, and Martha's bringing the props—she keeps all of that stored in a spare room at home, from what I hear."

Andrew clapped his hands together. "Alright, folks, if that's everything, we'll wrap it up here."

Andrew strolled toward their group, a broad grin lighting up his face.

"Oh no," Emma joked, raising a brow, "Andrew's thinking again."

Andrew grinned at her, his eyes alight with his usual mischief. "I was thinking maybe we could keep tonight's momentum going. How about we head back to my place for some pizza? We can order in, put our feet up—have a good evening catching up."

The idea sparked immediate chatter among the group. Leah leaned toward Emma, clearly on board. "This will be fun. Just like old times—minus Mom hollering at us to keep it down."

Mark lifted an amused brow as if to ask if she was in, and her resolve softened. Wendy nudged Emma's shoulder playfully, as if reminding her she had, after all, come here to reconnect.

"I'm in... it's not like I can really avoid it, seeing as I'm staying there for now," Emma teased with a smile. "But Andrew has to promise extra cheese on one of the pizzas. And since he's feeling so mischievous tonight, he can cover the tab as well."

"Consider it done." Andrew's quick response was far too enthusiastic, his grin stretching wide as he pretended to scribble notes on an imaginary clipboard. "And we'll throw in garlic knots because what's pizza without a side of garlic knots?"

Martha shook her head with a smile, her tiredness showing around the edges. "You kids go have fun. I need to get to bed, or I'll be falling asleep during the sermon tomorrow."

"Oh, we'll miss you, Martha!" Wendy chimed.

"We'll miss her keeping Andrew in line, more like it," Leah quipped.

"Let's head to the house, then!" Andrew declared, switching off the lights as the group filed toward the exit.

Outside, the cold bit at Emma's cheeks as wind brushed past, weaving around their scarves and jackets. The churchyard was peaceful, the snow that coated the ground shimmering faintly under the streetlights. They moved together, steps crunching against the frozen ground, breath leaving in icy puffs.

Mark fell in step next to her. He leaned in, offering his scarf when the wind picked up again.

"I'm fine," Emma said with a smile, wrapping her arms more snugly around herself.

His eyes held hers for a beat longer, something unspoken and kind passing between them in the silence, as peaceful as the snow falling gently around them. Then, from her other side, Olivia's small hand appeared, reaching up and wrapping itself around Emma's fingers.

"Miss Emma, look! The snow makes everything so sparkly! Just like the angel costume, right?"

Emma felt a warmth in her chest as Olivia looked up at her. "That's right, sweetie." She squeezed the tiny hand in hers, and they walked together, Olivia chattering about how excited she was for tomorrow's play rehearsal.

When they reached the parsonage, a glow radiated from the windows and the scent of evergreen carried on the breeze.

"Come on in, make yourselves at home!" Andrew called as everyone shuffled inside, brushing snow off their boots.

Emma slipped off her coat and smiled and watched as Mark helped Olivia remove hers.

Andrew worked on starting a fire in the hearth, and before long, with the flick of a match, soft orange flames danced across the room, casting gentle shadows on the walls.

"I'll start a pot of coffee," Emma said, moving toward the kitchen.

Andrew settled into one of the armchairs in the living room, putting his feet up on the ottoman. "I'll take mine black, if you don't mind," he added with a grin.

"Oh, anything for you, dear brother," Emma said with a smirk.

"Hot chocolate for me, please!" Olivia called from the couch, her voice mimicking the grown-ups around her.

Emma chuckled. "Coming right up." Sliding the kettle onto the stove, she grabbed a bag of cocoa mix, watching the steam begin to rise. She flipped the coffeepot on. Just as she reached for the mugs, she felt a slight tug at her sweater.

"Miss Emma?" Olivia was at her side, eyes full of curiosity. "Do you know how to make cookies? Really yummy cookies like Gigi does?"

"Gigi? I'm thinking that's your great-grandma, right?" Emma smiled down at the little girl. "I do know how to make cookies. What kind of cookies do you and Gigi make?"

Olivia tilted her head, fingers tapping at her chin. "We make peanut butter cookies. I get to roll the little balls of dough in sugar. Daddy says mine are the best." She grinned with pride.

"I bet they are," Emma encouraged, stirring the warm milk and setting the cocoa down in front of her. "Maybe you can teach me how to make them one day."

Olivia's face lit up at the suggestion. "Oh yes! Then we'll pray over them before they go in the oven, just like Gigi does. She always says, 'Lord bless that these bake properly, so they don't burn!'" Olivia giggled, and Emma found herself laughing too.

The sound of Mark clearing his throat met her ears, and she turned to see him standing in the doorway, watching the interaction.

"She's not bothering you, is she?" Mark asked, though the twinkle in his eyes said otherwise.

"Not at all," Emma replied with a smile, handing Olivia her mug. "We're having a very serious discussion about cookies."

"Well, in that case," Mark teased, "I'll leave you two to it."

She and Olivia returned to the living room, where the fire was now burning brightly, giving the room an almost magical glow. The pizzas arrived not long after, and soon they were spread out on the coffee table, laughter echoing throughout.

"Remember the Christmas caroling contest we got dragged into?" Leah said as she swatted Andrew's arm. "If it wasn't for Emma's high notes, we wouldn't have stood a chance!"

Emma rolled her eyes. "Oh, please. If you hadn't been singing in a windstorm of giggles, we might've actually won!"

The group burst into laughter, Olivia's eyes widening as she grabbed a slice of pizza, listening in awe. "Did you really sing songs, Miss Emma?"

"To the whole town," Andrew replied with a grin as he winked at Mark. "And Emma here—she had a crush on one certain boy in the choir. Took practicing in the church basement to a whole new level."

"Andrew!" Emma tossed her napkin at him, her cheeks instantly warming. With a brief, somewhat sheepish glance at Mark, she knew he probably remembered it, too.

Mark, who had been quietly listening, chuckled under his breath but caught Emma's eye with something almost like curiosity. His laughter was softer, as if trying to process the person Emma had been back then—the girl he knew then—and the woman sitting here now.

Olivia, her curiosity piqued, squirmed in closer. "Miss Emma, did you really have a crush on someone?"

Emma cleared her throat and tapped Olivia's nose playfully. "That's for another time, sweetheart."

Wendy chimed in with a grin, "Remember that time in high school when we were delivering the Blessing Baskets we made at church?"

"Oh, I remember that well. I'll never forget that," Leah chimed in.

"What happened?" Olivia asked, her wide eyes filled with eager curiosity.

Wendy leaned back in her chair, letting out a soft laugh. "Well, let me tell you, Olivia," she began, glancing at Emma with a mischievous grin. "It was the middle of December—just like now—and we'd spent weeks putting together Blessing Baskets for families all around Laurel Ridge. You know, bags filled with food, small toys, mittens, scarves, and all that good stuff."

Emma groaned but smiled, already knowing where this story was heading.

"And your Miss Emma," Leah added, smirking, "got it into her head that we should deliver them late at night, so everyone could wake up the next morning to a surprise by their front doors."

"I didn't want it to feel like charity," Emma interjected defensively, her eyes twinkling. "I thought it would be fun to leave the bags on the doorsteps like a secret Santa type gift. It was supposed to be a heartwarming surprise."

Wendy chuckled, lifting her hands in mock surrender. "True, but you didn't think about one small thing..."

"What happened next?" Olivia asked.

"A dog!" Leah exclaimed. "Turns out the house we were sneaking up to had the biggest, most terrifying dog you could imagine, and it wasn't exactly thrilled about five teenagers creeping around its porch in the middle of the night!"

Olivia gasped, wide-eyed. "Oh, no! What did you do?"

"I froze." Emma admitted, with a guilty laugh, playing with the hem of her sweater. "I stood there, basket in hand, when this huge dog—what was it? A German shepherd or something?" she asked, glancing toward Wendy.

Wendy nodded, wiping away a tear of laughter. "Yep. A massive German shepherd."

Emma nodded and continued. "So this dog, barking its head off like we were trying to rob the place, and me... instead of running, I just... stood there. Terrified."

Andrew, who had joined the conversation from his armchair, grinned. "It was the first time I'd ever seen Emma really freaked out. She usually kept her cool, but that dog? She was a statue."

"And meanwhile," Leah continued, "we're all yelling from the road, 'Run, Emma! Run!' But she wouldn't move! Just stood there, frozen stiff."

"And then your daddy couldn't hold back any longer, Olivia," Andrew said with a wide grin, "So he ran over, scooped Emma up, tossed her over his shoulder like a sack of potatoes, and sprinted back toward us."

Emma waved a hand, glancing at Olivia, who was listening with rapt attention. "Eventually, the owners opened the door, called the dog off, and we hand-delivered their basket after explaining to them why five teenagers were out sneaking around late at night."

Mark chuckled, shaking his head. "I remember that well."

"Good thing you didn't get bitten!" Olivia gasped, her hands covering her mouth as if the thought were just too wild to imagine.

"No bites," Emma reassured her. "Just my pride wounded."

"You were lucky!" Wendy added with a wink, "Some people in town still bring it up now and again. You did your good deed for the night, though."

Olivia, always curious and full of questions, tugged gently at her dad's sleeve. Her wide brown eyes twinkled with amusement as she tilted her head. "Daddy, did you really pick up Miss Emma like a sack of potatoes?"

Mark chuckled softly, the warmth of the memory flickering across his face. He looked over at Olivia, his smile widening. "I sure did, sweetheart," he said in his gentle, yet amused tone.

Emma grinned, feeling the warmth of nostalgia settle over her. These were the moments she had missed—the shared laughter, the stories passed around like treasured heirlooms. Glancing over at Mark, she found him already watching her, his expression gentle and unreadable.

Before she could dwell on it much longer, Olivia broke the silence with another eager question.

"Next time you deliver the Blessing Baskets, can I come too? I'll make sure to stay away from any dogs!" she exclaimed bravely, her chest puffing out with pride.

Emma laughed. "I'll hold you to that, Olivia."

"Remember that Christmas tree hunt back in our senior year, Emma?" Leah asked with a smile.

"That was such a good time," Emma said, nodding as she remembered.

"You went on a hunt for a Christmas tree?" Olivia asked, her eyes wide with curiosity.

"That's right," Andrew said. "Your daddy, me, Emma, Leah, and Wendy all set out to find the biggest Christmas tree we could for the church. It was just about this time of year, and your great-grandpa Eli was getting a little anxious because he hadn't had the chance to go out and find a tree for the recreation hall yet."

"So," Emma began with a playful twinkle in her eye, "we knew your great-grandpa was feeling a little impatient, so we decided to surprise him. We trekked through the hills, determined to find the tallest, grandest tree we could. We wandered for what felt like hours, laughing the whole time, and when we finally found it—well, it was a tree so big we weren't even sure we'd be able to bring it back!"

Emma laughed, glancing at Mark, who smiled warmly, clearly remembering the day.

"It took all of us working together," Leah added, leaning forward as if she were sharing a secret. "Andrew had the brilliant idea to tie ropes to the tree with what little rope we had, and then we all tried to haul it back to the truck."

Andrew smirked. "If I remember right, it was a good idea—until the rope snapped."

Olivia gasped, utterly enthralled. "Then what did you do?!"

Mark chuckled from his seat, interjecting, "Well, that's when some more bad luck hit—we realized we were completely lost. We had absolutely no idea how to get back to the road."

"No way!" Olivia exclaimed, her small hands clasped tightly, as if she were hanging on to every word said.

Laughing, Emma nodded. "Oh, it's true. We wandered in the dark for what felt like an eternity. And every time we stopped, the tree seemed to grow about five more inches."

"And every crack or rustle in the woods? We were sure it was a bear," Leah added with a grin.

"I wasn't worried about bears." Andrew joked, puffing his chest out in mock bravado. "But I do remember Wendy screaming when a raccoon ran across the trail—"

"—It ran right over my foot!" Wendy interjected with a laugh. "Even Mark jumped."

Mark opened his mouth to protest, but then just shook his head, grinning. "In my defense, I didn't expect a raccoon to appear out of nowhere in the dark."

Olivia's eyes were huge now, completely captivated. "Did you make it out of the woods?" she asked breathlessly.

Emma leaned toward Olivia, her voice soft but full of suspenseful mystery. "Well... it took us a few more hours, but yes, we made it. And the next day, when your Great-Grandpa Eli saw the tree, he was so happy and excited. He said it looked like something out of a fancy movie!"

Mark nodded, chuckling. "It really was quite the tree... once we cleaned all the mud and gunk off it."

"And decorated it with everything we could find in the church basement!" Wendy added, smiling at the memory.

Olivia sighed dreamily. "I wish I could've seen it! It sounds like the best Christmas tree ever."

Emma smiled, warmth spreading through her chest as Olivia's excitement bubbled over. "Well, how about this? Maybe one day soon we can all go out to find a tree together. What do you think, Olivia?"

The little girl's face lit up brighter than the Christmas lights. "Yes! Please! Daddy, can we? Can we really go tree hunting together?"

Mark chuckled softly, his gaze lingering on Emma for a moment before he turned to his daughter. "I think we can make that happen, Liv."

Olivia squealed and hugged Emma around the waist. "Thank you, Miss Emma!"

Chapter 12

Snow flurries twirled and danced gracefully in the cold air outside, their delicate shapes like tiny ornaments drifting on the breeze. Inside, the recreation hall was a hub of cozy warmth and lively activity. The soft murmur of conversation filled the space, harmonizing with the rustle of more boxes being unpacked and the joyful peals of children's laughter. The festive energy was infectious as everyone busied themselves with preparations for the upcoming children's Christmas play.

Emma shrugged off her coat, shivering slightly as the lingering chill of winter clung to her skin. A smile tugged at her lips as she took in the cozy scene—the congregation members gathered around tables, hands busy with holiday crafts and preparations for the upcoming play.

Around her, familiar faces brightened up the room—Wendy talking animatedly with Leah, Martha trying and failing to convince Andrew that the wise men's costumes really could do with her "Scottish plaid upgrade," and little clusters of parents helping their children into angel wings and shepherd outfits.

As she scanned the room, her gaze inevitably sought one particular face. As if sensing her presence, his eyes lifted, just for a moment—and in that small beat of hesitation, they locked onto hers.

A soft flush rose to her cheeks.

Emma, flustered by how easily the moment threw her off balance, took a breath and broke eye contact first. She busied herself untangling a string of Christmas lights gathered on the table in front of her—something to focus on to steady her pounding heart.

This is ridiculous, she thought, carefully untangling the lights. *You didn't come here to get flustered over glances and memories.*

But the way his quiet intensity lingered, mixed with that trace of old familiarity—it sent her mind spiraling back to last night. The warmth of the fire in the parsonage, pizza boxes spread out on the coffee table, and Olivia's delighted laughter filling the room. She hadn't felt that much at home in a long time, like she belonged again. Like she wasn't just drifting through life, but re-rooting herself in this little West Virginia corner of the world.

Suddenly, a flash of bright color caught her eye as Olivia ran over, her angel wings half-fastened, flapping. "Miss Emma!" she called, breathless with excitement. "I can't find my sparkly shoes! Have you seen them?"

Emma grinned, sinking down to Olivia's level. She gave the little girl's flyaway curls a gentle pat. "Hmm... I don't think sparkly shoes can just disappear, do you? Let's check under the table."

Olivia dropped to the floor without hesitation, peeking under the cloth-covered table in a determined attempt to solve the mystery. Emma knelt beside her.

She felt a presence behind her—warm and steady—and when she turned her head and looked back, Mark was standing nearby, watching with a tender smile.

"Looks like you've got a detective on your hands," Mark said, crossing his arms as if to keep himself from reaching out to help. His voice held that same warm tinge from the previous night—as if a tentative bridge was being built between them with each moment that passed.

Emma let out a soft chuckle, rising again from her crouched position. "Apparently so. Olivia's determined to find her sparkly shoes."

The little girl, now sprawled under another table with fierce concentration, chimed in, her voice muffled but still hopeful. "I'll find them! They can't hide forever!"

"They were in the costume bag yesterday, Olivia," Emma remembered. "Did you check there?"

Olivia popped up from under the table, her angel wings now even more askew. "Oh..." She giggled. "I forgot!"

Grinning, Mark shook his head. "I'd better go help her before those wings end up flying off entirely."

Emma smiled and nodded. "Go on. I'll be over here when you're ready."

Mark shot her a glance before turning to help his daughter. As Emma watched him move toward the pile of stage costumes, guiding Olivia with a gentle hand on her shoulder, a foreign feeling bloomed in her chest.

Lightness.

Hope.

Happiness.

It stirred deep within her, unexpected yet undeniably present.

She stopped, pulling back before the flutter in her heart could take flight. It was too soon—too risky—to allow herself to get caught up in this kind of thing again. After all, Mark had once been the one to walk out of her life when they were younger. He had ended things abruptly, leaving more questions than answers behind, and the quiet ache of that loss had lingered longer than she'd cared to admit.

No, she reminded herself. *That was years ago.*

People grow, people change—but some wounds, even when healed, leave scars. She needed to be careful, especially with the way her heart responded to someone who had already hurt it once before.

When Mark and Olivia returned—Olivia now fully decked out in sparkling shoes and wings, miraculously still intact—the rest of the group was already gathering for a proper rehearsal.

Andrew, clipboard in hand, paced back and forth near the small stage, laying out what remained to be done. "Alright," he said, clapping his hands together in typical Andrew fashion. "The nativity play should go off smoothly if everyone stays focused... Unlike last year, when the camel wandered off behind the stable and caused a five-minute long shepherding debacle."

Andrew's comment earned chuckles from the volunteers, particularly Martha, who had been the one to coax last year's rogue camel, Liam Sanders, back from behind the set.

Emma only half-listened to her brother as he prattled on about shepherd coordination tactics for the play. Her attention kept slipping back to Mark. He was seated beside her at the small table now, Olivia happily perched on a chair, flipping through a children's bible storybook she had retrieved from her backpack.

Mark shifted in his chair. Emma glanced over and was surprised to find him watching her, a quiet, contemplative look on his face.

"You okay?" she asked, keeping her voice low.

Mark's gaze dipped, and he let out a small breath to steady himself before replying. "Yeah, just... thinking."

Feeling bold, though unsure why, Emma leaned over slightly, curious. "Thinking about what?"

Mark hesitated, his hand tapping lightly on the table in front of him, as if weighing his words carefully. "Mostly about Olivia... and this coming Christmas."

"What's on your mind?" Emma asked, her voice soft but curious.

"Well, you did mention to Olivia last night that we could all go on a Christmas tree hunt together," Mark said with a playful grin. "And you know how kids are—they never forget things like that. Especially Olivia. She's been reminding me every day that we still need to get a tree. So don't be surprised if she starts poking at you about it, too."

Emma chuckled, warmth spreading through her chest at the thought of Olivia's persistence. "I have a feeling I'll be hearing about this tree hunt for quite a while. I should be careful with my promises."

Mark smiled. "When she's excited, she knows how to keep you true to your word. But honestly, I'd like it if you came along when we go to pick out our tree."

Emma glanced toward the stage, where Olivia was now practicing her angel performance, her little wings askew and Martha trying to adjust them.

She looked back at Mark, seeing the gentle hope in his eyes, and the hesitation she felt melted away.

"Okay," she said, her voice firm with a decision she hadn't expected making so soon. "Let's do it. I'll help you find the perfect Christmas tree."

Mark's face softened into a smile—with a hint of something deeper, something unspoken yet undeniable. "Our last tree hunt together was... memorable."

Emma laughed. "I think we'll manage just fine this time, too."

Mark reached over and placed his hand on Emma's, causing her pulse to quicken.

Their eyes met, and for a moment, the busy chatter of the hall seemed to fade away.

***

After another round of prop organizing and costume adjustments, the group was beginning to wind down for the afternoon. The children—all rattled from the rehearsal—gathered around the small snack tables by the windows, enjoying cookies and cider Martha had brought from the diner. Laughter filled the room as children and toddlers toddled about in their costumes, still adorned with shepherd headpieces and glittering tinsel halos.

Mark made his way over from the snack table, two cups of warm cider in hand. Handing one to Emma, he took a seat beside her near the window, where the soft, fading light of the wintry afternoon made the room feel cozier.

"You did great today," Mark said as he took a sip of his cider, nodding toward the bustling group toward the front of the room. "I think you're going to be the reason this play turns out better than we ever expected."

Emma laughed, shaking her head. "Oh, I doubt that. You've seen these kids—they have so much enthusiasm, they're practically doing all the work themselves."

"Well," Mark grinned, "you're modest. But you're doing something good here, Emma."

His words hit something deep. They were simple, yes—but spoken with such sincerity that Emma had to pause and collect her thoughts, carefully protected behind a smile.

"I really needed this," she admitted quietly, almost to herself. "I needed to come home."

Mark studied her, something thoughtful lingering on his face before he spoke again. "You know... pops, Eli, that is, that's what I call him, always says, 'God's paths are rarely straightforward—but they're always the right ones.'" He chuckled slightly, shaking his head.

Emma's throat tightened, pieces of their broken lives still hovering between them like unfinished chapters.

"Do you think..." she started, her voice hesitant but vulnerable. "Do you think there's a reason we're both here together again? After all this time?"

Mark's brows furrowed slightly, his earthy-brown eyes holding hers with an intensity she wasn't ready for.

"I don't know anything about God's plans, Emma," he said, "but I'd be lying if I said it didn't feel like something brought us back together. You being here... it feels right."

Olivia came bounding toward them, her energy contagious. The little girl wrapped herself around Emma in a tight hug.

"Miss Emma," Olivia asked, her brown eyes sparkling with excitement, "do you think we could go find our Christmas tree now?"

Emma's eyes flickered toward Mark's

"Not today, sweetheart," Mark said gently, leaning forward to look Olivia in the eye. "Remember, the tree farm is closed on Sundays. We'll have to wait just a little while longer."

"Can't we go on a hike like you used to when you were younger and find one in the woods?" Olivia asked eagerly.

"Well," Mark began with a gentle smile, "we could, but your legs might not last the whole hike. We'd need to trek pretty far into the mountains to find the perfect tree."

Olivia, undeterred by her dad's answer, quickly shifted gears. "Well, can Miss Emma come home with us, then?" She turned toward

Emma, her expressive brown eyes shining with hope. "Grandma and I are decorating Christmas cookies today. Would you like to come?"

Emma looked between Olivia and Mark, feeling a flutter of warmth at the little girl's innocent invitation.

Mark's eyes met hers, soft and inviting, but with no pressure—just a quiet nod, as if to say that they'd be glad to have her. But it was her choice entirely.

She smiled at Olivia, her decision made.

"Well," Emma said, "I'd never say no to decorating cookies with the best little girl in town. Lead the way."

Olivia beamed, her excitement bubbling up as she looked at her dad. "Daddy, Miss Emma's coming! We're going to have the best cookie decorating day ever!"

Mark laughed, his warm gaze shifting to Emma once more. "Looks like it's settled, then."

"I just need to swing by the house and change clothes first," Emma said, a slight smile on her lips. "Where should I head after that?"

Mark smiled. "Remember where Pop and Grandma's place is?"

She nodded, the memory of their old family home clear in her mind.

"I live nearby," he explained. "We share the same driveway. It forks off a bit to the right where mine starts. You'll know it when you see it."

Emma chuckled softly. "Got it. I'll be about fifteen minutes behind you."

"Take your time," Mark replied, his gaze warm as he returned her smile.

As they gathered their things to leave the recreation hall, Emma's mind drifted to the past, slipping back into memories she hadn't meant to revisit again. Seeing Mark like this—laughing, offering her warm smiles, gently nudging her into his world—made it all too easy to forget how things had ended between them all those years ago. She couldn't allow herself to overlook that fact. The pull to be a part of his life again felt magnetic, almost inevitable, but Emma knew better than to trust that pull without caution.

She'd loved Mark once—deeply, completely. But loving him had also meant grappling with the stinging pain of how abruptly he'd walked out of her life. No explanation, no real clarity, just... distance. One day, they had been planning their lives together, talking about dreams and places they'd see, and the next, he'd disappeared like a ghost, leaving her with a heart full of questions that had never been answered.

Even now, years later, the sharp edges of that hurt hadn't dulled completely. Sure, she'd moved on—or had tried to, at least. She had built her life in Pittsburgh, immersed herself in her career, found love with Rhett... but a part of her had never fully healed from the way Mark had ended things. Why had he pulled away so suddenly? What had caused him to turn his back on what they had? She'd never gotten the answer she deserved, and that unanswered question lingered like a bruise beneath the surface.

As she watched him now, doing his best to raise Olivia with steady hands and a hopeful heart, Emma couldn't deny a deep respect for the man he'd become. But there was still hurt inside her—one she wasn't sure she could ignore. Mark owed her an explanation. She wasn't expecting an apology; years had passed, and life had taught her that people made choices they didn't always know how to explain at the time. But she deserved to understand why he had walked away, why he had disappeared, leaving her to pick up the pieces.

Emma sighed, willing her heart to stay centered. She could feel herself opening the door to forgiveness, could feel the stirrings of something new—but this time, if she were to move forward with Mark, she needed to take it slow. Deliberate. She couldn't just jump into his life, no matter how much Olivia's sweetness or Mark's gentle presence drew her in. She deserved more than that—she deserved honesty and clarity. And Mark would have to be willing to give both before she could let him in again. There was too much at stake for all of them.

As they made their way outside, Olivia practically skipping between them, Emma reminded herself to be cautious. She wasn't that same love struck girl anymore, content to overlook everything because her heart wanted to believe in the fairy tale. The road ahead might carry the promise of rekindled warmth, but it would only work if they were honest about the past. And until she got the explanation she deserved, her heart would remain guarded—even as it stretched toward the possibility of forgiveness and new beginnings.

Chapter 13

Emma pulled her SUV into the long, winding driveway of Mark's home, her breath catching at the sight before her. The cabin looked like something straight from a holiday postcard, nestled cozily within the snow-draped landscape. The last traces of daylight clung to the horizon, painting the snow in soft lavender and blush hues. Twinkling lights hung along the porch roof, swaying gently in the breeze, their pale blue and white glow casting a festive warmth against the growing dusk.

It was her first time visiting Mark's home, though the property itself was familiar. Years ago, she'd often come to visit Eli and Claire's house, which was just down the way. Back then, Mark had lived with his parents farther down the road, back in their simpler high school days. So much has changed since then. Now, Mark's home stood beautiful and perfectly in tune with the natural surroundings.

Emma could easily imagine how peaceful it must be living so close to Eli and Claire. She had always adored their gentle nature and the warmth they filled their home with. Mark's house before her now—rustic, charming, and welcoming—felt like an extension of that warmth.

Emma's tires crunched against the snow packed gravel driveway as she came to a stop and turned off the ignition. Her heart beat a bit faster than usual, a mix of nerves and excitement. It wasn't just the idea of decorating Christmas cookies with Olivia that had her feeling this way. It was stepping into a world, the world of Mark and his family, which was familiar yet different.

She opened the door and stepped out into the cold evening air. Before she could even close her car door behind her, a small figure dashed toward her, giggles floating above the snow.

"Miss Emma! You came!" Olivia shrieked, her voice high with excitement as she ran toward Emma, her boots stamping down eager little footprints in the snow.

"I told you I'd be here, didn't I?" Emma smiled, her heartwarming at the bubbly seven-year-old, who had now thrown herself into Emma's arms for an enthusiastic hug.

Olivia squeezed tightly and then pulled back, bouncing on her toes. "Come on, come on! Daddy said we could start decorating cookies after you got here!"

"Well, I'd hate to keep cookies waiting!" Emma chuckled. She took Olivia's hand as they hurried toward the porch, her breath swirling into small clouds from the cold.

The front door creaked open, and Mark stood waiting on the threshold, a smile carved onto his face that sent a ripple of warmth through Emma. There was something about his rugged appearance—dark jeans, flannel shirt—that felt both familiar and new, like an old friend seen through fresh eyes.

"Glad you made it," Mark said. "Olivia's been waiting by the window for the last ten minutes."

"I have not, Daddy!" Olivia burst out in defense, although her grin betrayed her. Then she rushed ahead, bouncing through the door like energy bottled in a tiny package.

Emma laughed and stepped onto the porch, brushing off some snow from her boots by the door.

Mark's home was a sight to behold—a true, authentic log cabin. The first thing that struck Emma as she stepped inside was the immediate sense of timeless charm that enveloped her. The whole place felt as though it had been carefully curated to blend comfort with the rugged beauty of its natural surroundings, creating a haven of both coziness and tranquility.

To her right, the living room beckoned with its rich, earthy tones—deep burgundies, forest greens, and deep blues. Dominating the far wall was a large stone fireplace, its hearth sprawling from floor to ceiling. The flickering flames crackled softly, casting an amber light across the room and filling the air with the unmistakable scent of burning wood. It was the centerpiece of the space, exuding both strength and serenity.

Arranged in a semicircle around the fire was a plush wraparound sofa, large enough to gather family and friends alike, while two oversized recliners sat on either side like sentinels of relaxation, their cushioned arms soft and inviting. The furniture was simple yet elegant, upholstered in textures that invites one to sink in deeply, perhaps with a book in hand or simply sit quietly before the fire's hypnotic dance.

On the mantle, old photographs in rustic wooden frames offered glimpses into Mark's life—images of him with Olivia and his grandparents over the years, family portraits of Mark, Maggie and a young Olivia, as well as scenic shots of Laurel Ridge through the seasons.

Handmade quilts draped over the back of the recliners, adding layers of warmth and history—each stitch, a testament to love, patience, and family traditions. Soft, knitted throws were casually spread over the armrests of the wraparound sofa.

The room had a lived-in feel—a space created for shared laughter, warm conversations, and moments of quiet reflection.

"Here," Mark said, stepping forward and extending a hand, "Let me take your coat."

Emma paused for a second. She felt flustered at first, but then offered a grateful smile. "Thank you."

Claire appeared from the kitchen with a soft smile on her face, her gray hair pulled into an easy bun, and her apron was already delicately dusted with powdered sugar. "Emma, it's so wonderful to see you."

"It's good to see you too, Mrs. Thompson," Emma said, feeling the welcome permeate every corner of the room.

"None of this Mrs. Thompson business. You've known me long enough, dear. It's Clair," she said, waving off the formality with a hand.

Emma gave a soft laugh, the ease of Clair's kindness settling on whatever nerves she had left. Clair stepped forward, drawing her into a quick embrace, before pulling back and inspecting Emma with a fond but appraising eye.

"I saw you and Eli in church this morning, and I'm sorry I didn't get a chance to speak with you then," Emma said.

"Nonsense Emma. You were busy speaking with the other members, no worries.... You know you've gotten even more beautiful through the years," Clair said softly, with a maternal smile. "I'm excited about decorating cookies with you and Olivia this evening."

Emma chuckled. "Well, I'm not the most creative cookie decorator, but I'll do my best."

"No worries. We just have fun. None of us are perfectionists!" Clair replied. She gave Emma's shoulder a light squeeze and then turned back toward the kitchen. "Come on in. Cookies won't frost themselves."

From his chair at the kitchen table, Eli gave an approving nod, his gentle eyes sparkling. "Good to see you back in Laurel Ridge, Emma. Brings back good memories."

Emma moved closer to Eli, feeling the weight of history wash over her. His voice was soft but carried all the authority and wisdom years of preaching had earned him. She smiled and leaned in to hug him. "It's good to be back, Mr. Thompson. Really good."

Eli grinned, his eyes full of quiet knowing. "I've missed you," he said.

"Miss Emma, come over here!" Olivia called. "Daddy said we can use all the sprinkles and glitter we want!"

She was bouncing on her toes. Her whole face lit up like a Christmas tree as she orchestrated the cookie decorating with all the authority of a commander leading troops.

Emma moved toward the kitchen island, letting Olivia's vibrant energy whirl her into the moment. Neatly arranged on the counter were cookies in all shapes—angels, trees, snowflakes—waiting to be adorned. Bowls of frosting in pastel shades and enough sprinkles and glitter to rival a candy store were set up whimsically, ready to be turned into cookie magic.

Clair handed Emma an apron. She slipped it over her head and tied it snugly around her waist, feeling a flutter of anticipation.

"Ready to dive in?" Clair asked playfully.

Laughing softly, Emma nodded. "Absolutely. Let's see if I still remember how to have a little cookie decorating fun."

Mark chuckled as he grabbed a small spatula from the counter. Catching Emma's eye, as he grinned. "Don't let her trick you into over-decorating. She has a thing for sprinkles and edible glitter."

Emma laughed, brushing her sleeves back as she accepted the spatula. "Something tells me Olivia has strong ideas about cookie aesthetics," she said as she glanced down at the cookies waiting to become edible artwork. "I'll do my best not to throw a glitter party on each one."

Mark chuckled, leaning against the counter next to her. His nearness didn't exactly make things easier. His laughter, his presence—it all made Emma's heart turn just a bit unsteady.

Olivia tugged at Emma's apron, drawing her attention, holding a sugar angel cookie triumphantly. "This one! This one's the best one and it's for you!" she declared. "I wore angel wings, like this, at play practice today!"

Emma smiled, smoothing Olivia's curls softly. "You sure did, and you were the prettiest little angel."

Olivia beamed, her whole face lighting up with excitement. Emma couldn't help but notice the way Olivia allowed joy to overflow in every moment—the kind of joy that saw wonder in something as simple as sprinkles on a cookie. She bit back the rush of emotions that momentarily threatened to sweep her away.

"Well, no time to waste, Miss Emma," Mark said, looking down at the glittering angel cookie in Olivia's hand. "You heard the boss; this one's all yours."

The room filled with conversation and laughter. Mark had joined Eli at the kitchen table, and they had started chatting about the church Christmas play.

"You know, Emma," Clair said after a while, taking a bite of one of Olivia's freshly frosted stars, "I'm so glad you've come home. I've been missing some Whitman representation in our Christmas traditions."

Emma chuckled, brushing some sprinkles from the counter with her hand. "I've missed being here with you as well. It's funny," she said, pausing to glance thoughtfully at the snow falling outside, illuminated by the back porch lights, "how coming back feels like settling into something I didn't realize I was missing so much. Even though... everything's changed."

Clair leaned over with a soft look in her eyes. "Seems to me, honey, that God's been making those changes to bring you right back here again."

Eli nodded. "Home has a way of doing that. Sneaking back into your heart when you least expect it," he said.

Emma swallowed back the emotion that wanted to surface. "Yeah... home." She swirled some more red icing onto a snowman cookie, keeping her attention half on her work and half on what was being unsaid. She glanced back up at Mark.

His eyes penetrated her, and for a heartbeat, the room stilled, and she felt the connection between them—that they were on parallel journeys. Two people who had loved and lost, now finding themselves brought back together for reasons only God could understand.

Olivia burst into laughter, frosting smeared across her nose as she held up a cookie covered in pink sprinkles. "Daddy! Miss Emma! Look at this one! It's going to be Santa's cookie!"

Emma grinned, grateful for the change of pace. "That's a top-tier Santa cookie, Olivia. No one can beat your skills."

Olivia beamed as she tugged gently on her hand. "Let's make this our special cookie for Santa—since you're helping me tonight, it can be from both of us!"

A warm feeling spread through Emma's chest as she bent down to Olivia's level. "I supposed that sounds like a great idea."

As the evening carried on, Clair, ever gracious and thoughtful, glided over to where Emma was tidying up some of the cookie decorations.

With her soft silver hair neatly pinned back and her eyes twinkling with curiosity, she struck up another conversation.

"So, Emma," Clair began, pulling out a chair and sitting down beside her with effortless ease. "Now that you've settled back into town, have you started thinking about where you want to live? I imagine Andrew's been happy to have you around the parsonage for now, but surely, you're planning to find a place of your own, eventually." Her tone carried both an easy familiarity and a hint of motherly care, as if she was already mentally arranging Emma's furniture for her.

"Well, for now, I'm grateful to have his company, but I haven't really made any decisions yet beyond that." She fiddled with the spoon in her hand, the metal tapping lightly against the edge of a cookie tray. "I want to find a place of my own, but I might just stay with Andrew until the weather warms up a little. You know how brutal winter can be—moving in snow and ice doesn't exactly sound like a fun adventure."

Clair chuckled, but she didn't let the subject drop. "True, true. And you have plenty of time to figure it all out. Perhaps wait a few months for spring to arrive... Laurel Ridge comes alive then. Everything blooming—flowers, hearts, and dreams alike. There's something about springtime in these mountains... I'm sure you remember."

Emma's smile widened, loving the poetic flair in Clair's voice. It felt almost like a lullaby to her soul, reassuring her that patience, not pressure, was the way forward. "Springtime is wonderful here," she said.

Clair's eyes softened, a knowing look gracing her face. "You'll find the right place when the time is perfect, Emma. Maybe not right away. And that's okay. To be honest," Clair leaned in just a touch closer, her voice dropping to a secretive whisper, "the best homes have a way of finding you, not the other way around."

Emma chuckled and shook her head, but the thought stayed with her. So much had been out of her control the past year—so much of her life had felt as though it had slipped through her fingers, like sand in the wind—but Clair's words were a subtle reminder of faith. Of allowing things to happen when they were supposed to.

"And remember when you find a place of your own to call home," Clair added with a smile. "Everyone around town will be eager to help, whether you ask for it or not. One mention after church, and I promise half the neighborhood will show up with paint supplies and casserole dishes ready to get you moved in."

Emma laughed at the thought. Laurel Ridge truly was a place of community, a town where people gathered when you needed them most, even in ways you didn't expect.

"I don't doubt that," Emma replied, taking a sip of her cooling hot cocoa. "I'm really glad to be back home. I've missed everyone so much."

Mark, who had been listening to the exchange between Clair and Emma, finally spoke. His voice was low, gentle, but serious. "Laurel Ridge—it has a way of holding onto people. Especially the ones it needs most."

Emma didn't know what to say. There was a depth to Mark's words that stirred something in her chest, a reminder of all that had passed between them years ago, and all that had been left unspoken.

Olivia squealed in delight as she held up a cookie she had absolutely smothered in blue icing and rainbow sprinkles. "Look, Daddy! It's a snowflake!" she announced proudly.

Mark smiled at her. "That's a masterpiece, Peanut," he said, crossing the room to crouch beside his daughter. He kissed her on the head, and a soft pang tugged at Emma's heart. It was such a simple act of parental love, yet the ease and warmth with which Mark embraced fatherhood only added to her emotions.

Clair cleared her throat softly, pulling Emma's attention back. "You know, Emma," she said with gentle affection, "we've missed you more than you realize."

Emma felt her breath hitch slightly, unsure how to respond.

"Grandma, would you mind keeping an eye on Olivia while Emma and I sit in the living room a little bit? I'd like to talk with her alone, if you wouldn't mind," Andrew asked.

Clair looked up from her task with a knowing smile, her eyes sparkling with warmth and good humor. "Of course, dear," she replied, brushing a streak of flour from her apron. "You two go ahead and chat." She winked in Emma's direction, her subtle encouragement palpable in the air.

"Don't you worry about a thing. Olivia and I will be just fine, won't we, sweetie?" she added, turning her attention back to Olivia, who was enthusiastically sticking sprinkles onto another snowman cookie following no particular pattern.

Olivia barely looked up, too engrossed in her masterpiece. "Yep!"

Mark smiled, grateful for his grandmother's ever-consistent support and patience. He glanced over at Emma, giving her a small nod. She hesitated for a brief moment, a light flutter in her chest as the evening's relaxed atmosphere shifted. She set down the towel she'd used to clean up a bit of frosting and followed Mark's lead.

Chapter 14

Mark motioned to the large cushioned sofa across from the fireplace in the living room. "Let's sit. I've been meaning to talk to you about something for a while now."

Emma gave a small, understanding nod and settled into one of the deep, plush cushions. She couldn't shake the feeling that something important was about to be said. There was gravity in his voice—a curtain, perhaps, finally ready to be pulled back.

For a moment, silence drifted between them, soft but full of something unsaid. Emma instinctively glanced toward the fire, the flames casting gentle flickers of gold, their uneven rhythm adding to her nerves.

Mark leaned forward on the couch, resting his hands on his knees, eyes fixed momentarily on the floor before meeting hers. "I've been wanting to talk to you... about how things ended between us all those years ago."

A slight knot formed in Emma's chest. Her fingers twitched in her lap. She nodded, keeping her gaze steady.

Mark hesitated, his hands flexing, as though preparing himself for the weight of his words. His voice was quieter than usual when he spoke, like a confession he'd been holding for years. "I'm not proud of how I handled things back then—how I just... walked away. I left without really explaining, and that's haunted me."

His voice broke off as he exhaled deeply, a sound laden with his discomfort. When his eyes found hers again, they held a vulnerability Emma hadn't seen in a long time. "I thought maybe if I just... disappeared, it would make things easier for both of us. Especially with all the pressure you were facing—college, moving, your dreams for the future... and me? I honestly didn't know where I fit in."

Emma sat quietly, her breath shallow. The memories rushed back—the long nights waiting for his calls, the unanswered questions she carried like a lead weight on her chest.

Mark's gaze dropped again. His voice fell to a whisper. "I was scared, Emma."

The knot in her chest loosened, just slightly, but it didn't melt entirely.

He continued, voice tight with regret, "You had such incredible dreams—dreams that reached far beyond what I could offer you. And me? I felt... small and unworthy. I was stuck, uncertain about my future. No career plan, no idea how to build something meaningful for myself, or for us. In my mind, I convinced myself you were better off without me—better off free. I figured I was just holding you back."

Emma's heart trembled at his words. All this time, she had wondered why—why he'd pushed her away, why everything had unraveled when it seemed like they were on the cusp of forever. Now, hearing his side laid bare, she wasn't sure if it hurt more or less.

Mark looked her in the eyes then, unflinching. He was rooted in the moment, determined. "What I didn't realize," he said, his voice tinged with emotion, "was that I didn't have the right to decide that. I didn't have the right to choose for you. I should've talked to you about how I was feeling. We should've faced it together. But instead, I ran, thinking I was sparing both of us from future pain."

Emma swallowed, the emotion building in her throat. "And by running... you ended up hurting us both more."

He nodded, his gaze softening but laden with regret. "I know. I should've been braver. But I didn't know how."

For a long moment, neither of them spoke. The silence lingered, stretching between them like a safety net—catching all the hurt that floated through the room. The fire crackled in the background, its flickers dancing with an ease that belied the tension between them.

Emma's hands clenched together as she absorbed his words, the rawness of his confession tugging at something long hidden. "For years," she said finally, her voice quieter than she intended, "I tried so hard to understand. I replayed that summer over and over in my mind, wondering what I could've done differently, why you had just broken up with me so suddenly and then... you vanished. I thought maybe I wasn't enough. I felt like I was to blame for pushing too hard or for not seeing what you needed. I even wondered if you had found someone else."

Mark's face winced slightly, as if feeling the sting of her words. "It wasn't anything you did, and no, there wasn't anyone else," he said.

"Back then, I carried so much guilt, so much unresolved hurt. When I was in college trying to move forward, I couldn't shake the feeling that part of me stayed behind, stuck in that last conversation we had." Emma said.

Mark looked at her, the weight of his gaze steady and deep. "I'm sorry, Emma. Truly. I wish I could undo the pain and hurt I caused you."

She nodded, blinking back the sting of tears. "Thank you," she said softly. The words were delicate, like a fragile truce, but they held plenty within them—mended wounds, a chance for understanding.

Mark let out a long breath, his fingers tapping against the couch, a physical release of the weight he'd been carrying for far too long.

After a beat of silence, Emma's curiosity kicked in. She glanced sideways at him before speaking. "So... you left, but what happened next? Where did you go?"

Mark's eyes flicked toward the flames, his mind wandering to another time. His hands fidgeted absently with the stitching on the cushion beneath him. "I went north for a bit," he said. "An old buddy of mine was living outside Charleston, and he had a spare bedroom. I thought I could figure things out—make sense of where I was headed in life."

Emma remained quiet, allowing him to continue at his own pace.

"For a while, I drifted through life," Mark admitted. His voice softened as the truth spilled forward. "I took odd jobs here and there, never anything permanent. I tried so hard to figure out what to do with my life... to figure out what my purpose was. And honestly, I was so empty inside. I thought if I put distance between myself and everything back home, the guilt from breaking up with you would disappear... but it didn't."

He chuckled bitterly, glancing toward her with a crooked smile. "You ever find yourself thinking life's supposed to feel freer when you aren't tied down, but then realize you're more lost than free?"

Emma nodded, feeling that ache of recognition settle in her chest.

Mark's gaze wandered again for a moment, searching. "No matter where I was or what distraction I chased after, you and... life back here at home stayed with me."

She raised her brow, not sure how to interpret that.

His voice was quieter when he added, "I missed you something fierce. Deep down, I knew breaking up with you had been a mistake. In fact... I knew it the minute I drove away and headed to Charleston."

There was a long pause before Mark spoke again, his voice heavy with thoughts of years gone by. "Eventually, home called me back. I walked into my parents' house after months of wandering. And for the first time in months, I breathed easier—like I'd been holding my breath the entire time I was away. And Dad said something that stuck with me—he reminded me that sometimes we have to stop running long enough to let God catch up."

"I got a job at the lumber mill nearby," Mark continued. "Pops took me under his wing, taught me the ropes, but more than that, he reminded me of who I was. He reminded me we don't build a life by running—only by rooting ourselves when it feels hardest to do so."

Emma mulled over his words, imagining a younger, more restless Mark walking away from his family and friends and the only life he had known.

Mark rubbed a hand over his face, leaning back slightly. "My family encouraged me to go to college or a trade school. And before long, I applied to attend college. I originally thought I'd become an architect like your dad. But, the architect's dream? It wasn't mine. I realized I wanted to teach children. I wanted to be that person in a child's life that made a lasting impression."

Emma smiled. "Makes sense," she said softly. "You always enjoyed helping with any of the youth programs at church, and you were good at it."

A brief flash of something softer flickered across Mark's face. But before he could say anything, Emma leaned in, voice hesitant but curious. "And Maggie... how did she fit into your life after all that?"

Mark's jaw tightened just enough to be noticeable. "I met her in college. She was brilliant—an engineering major. We hit it off fast. After we graduated, we got married and eventually moved back here. A little while later, Olivia came along."

There was a stretch of sobriety in his tone now, like the steeliness of recalling something too delicate to touch overtly. Emma stayed quiet, letting him tell it as he needed.

"She was everything to me," Mark continued, his voice rougher. "But life has a way of throwing you more storms than you ever think you can handle. Maggie got sick before Olivia was even out of her toddler years. Cancer."

Mark swallowed tightly, his voice lowering further. "She fought harder than anyone I've ever known. Two years. But... we lost her."

The room fell silent for a heartbeat too long, and Emma held herself steady, her mind flashing through the unimaginable struggles he had endured.

"We've both faced so much," Emma said softly, her voice laced with empathy. "But watching Olivia... it's clear how much love you've poured into her life. She's such a bright, beautiful soul, Mark—that's all you."

Mark smiled, his gaze briefly dropping as if to shield the depth of his emotions. "I don't know about that. I've just been trying to keep her grounded and give her a good life." He shook his head, exhaling slowly, before his voice softened to nearly a whisper. "But thank you."

For a moment, they just sat there, the weight of their shared pasts hanging in the air like freshly fallen snow—soft, but undeniable. When Mark looked up, his eyes were filled with something warm, yet tinged with the vulnerability he couldn't quite hide.

"We've both been carrying things for a while now—things that have shaped us," he said. "Tell me about you. What happened after you went off to college?"

Emma hesitated, her fingers tracing the edge of the cushion below her as memories flooded back. Talking about her life, those college years and beyond felt daunting, like pulling layers off an old wound that still hadn't fully healed. But there was something in Mark's gaze—gentle, unjudging—that nudged her to open up.

"You really hurt me when you broke things off with me and disappeared. After you left, I threw myself into school," she began. "I needed to focus on my future, on becoming someone I could be proud of. I was determined to build a life that had meaning. I wanted to make the world a little brighter."

She paused, exhaling softly. "Nursing felt right from the start. I loved the idea of helping people, of being the person who could offer comfort when all else seemed lost. And I did well. But you know how sometimes success feels... hollow?" She glanced at him, her expression wistful. "I had so many things going in the right direction for myself in Pittsburgh—the job, the city life, all the things I thought I wanted. But it never felt—"

"Like home," Mark finished, his voice a quiet echo of understanding.

Emma nodded, offering a soft, thoughtful smile, though there was sadness behind it. "Yeah... It never really felt like home. Something was always missing. No matter how many career milestones I hit, whether it was a pay raise or buying my townhouse—none of it ever really made me happy. It was like I was chasing something, but I didn't know what anymore." Her voice softened as she recalled the emptiness that lingered beneath the surface. "For years, I couldn't open myself up to anyone, not entirely. I was too afraid. Afraid of letting someone in, of having my heart broken again. So instead, I buried myself in work. Long hours at the hospital, picking up extra shifts... anything to fill the void." She trailed off, her gaze flickering briefly, as if the weight of those choices still clung to her like the morning mist.

"Then I met Rhett," she continued. "He was a doctor, new to the hospital—transferred from another state. He was charming, confident... and so full of life. You couldn't help but smile when you were around him. Tall, blonde hair, with this laugh that felt like sunshine after a storm. We clicked. It wasn't long before he started talking about the future."

Emma's gaze dropped momentarily as the memories surged forward. "He wanted to settle down. Marriage, house, everything... but I kept... hesitating. I told him I needed more time, that I wasn't ready yet, but the truth is, I was scared. Scared of opening my heart all the way."

She swallowed, feeling the familiar twinge in her chest. "Eventually, he proposed again... and I said yes. But even while planning the wedding, part of me was holding back. Like my heart couldn't completely let go and trust. Deep down, I wondered if there was something wrong with me... something that made me stay guarded and weary. I didn't fully understand it back then. I told myself it was just wedding jitters."

Emma paused, glancing over at Mark, her blue eyes filled with a mix of vulnerability and reflection. "Looking back, maybe I was just... scared. Terrified, really, of what it would mean to let someone in after everything between you and me. And Rhett... well, I think he sensed it. The subtle distance between us. I loved him, I did... but there was always this invisible wall."

Emma exhaled slowly, her fingers toying with the edge of her sleeve. "Then came the accident. That night... we were driving back from a friend's engagement party. It was snowing hard, but Rhett insisted he could handle it. And I trusted him. Then everything happened so fast, it's a blur. Bright headlights, screeching tires, and the sound of metal... crashing."

Her voice broke for a moment, but she held herself steady, pushing through the ache. "I woke up in the hospital. He never woke up at all."

"I'm so sorry, Emma," he said, his eyes glistening as if he could feel her pain alongside her, even though his own tragedy had unfolded differently.

Emma swallowed the lump in her throat, her fingers twisting together in her lap. "You learn to keep going, you know," she said, her voice trembling slightly. "One day at a time, right? But after... after that happened, Pittsburgh—everything about my life there—it just felt too heavy. Just too much. The noise, the city life... but mostly the memories. I didn't know how to move forward after Rhett's death. I felt like I was constantly trying to inch ahead, only to fall back. I felt stuck. And I was so tired... so very tired."

Mark leaned forward, his elbows resting on his knees as he listened intently. "That's why you came back to Laurel Ridge," he said, as though it all finally made sense.

"Yeah," Emma replied, the corners of her mouth softening into a sad smile. "Mom called me one day and told me about the school nurse position opening up, and... well, the idea of moving back home and starting over felt safe. It felt right."

Mark nodded, silently processing everything Emma had shared. His gaze flickered over to Olivia, who was still happily engrossed in her cookie decorations with Clair in the kitchen still, and then back to Emma.

"I'm glad you came back," he said, his voice laced with sincerity.

"I'm glad I came back too," she said. "Do you think we can ever really... heal from the past?" she asked, not entirely sure who she was asking—herself, Mark, or maybe even God.

Mark leaned back a bit, his eyes fixed on the glow of the fire as the flames licked the edges of the logs, crackling softly. "I think," he said slowly, choosing his words with care, "that healing isn't something that happens all at once. Grief... loss... they stay with you. But they don't have to define you. I've come to believe that God doesn't just heal by taking the pain away, but by walking through it with us, showing us that we're never alone—and sometimes, He brings people back into our lives who help guide us the rest of the way." He glanced back at her then, his brown eyes warm and patient.

Emma looked at him. "Maybe you're right," she said, almost as though agreeing with herself more than anyone else. "Maybe coming home wasn't just about finding comfort... maybe it was about finding the courage to face my heart again."

Mark's brow lifted slightly. "And is that what you're doing?" he asked gently.

"Trying," she admitted quietly, the word heavier than she'd meant it to sound. "Rhett's memory is still with me, just like Maggie is for you. But... being here, back in this town, with you, Olivia, Andrew, and everyone else... it's helping me remember what it feels like to hope again."

Mark smiled, his gaze thoughtful as he searched her face. "Hope's a powerful thing, Emma. It can be fragile at first, but once it takes root, it grows stronger every day."

She looked at him, feeling that seed of hope stirring in her chest. It was still small, still tender, but it was there, and that was enough for now. She could feel it—the soft possibility of joy after sorrow, of belonging after feeling lost. There were no easy answers, no guarantees, but there was a chance for healing and new beginnings.

They sat in companionable silence for a while. The fire crackling softly in front of them as the room filled with the quiet hum of Olivia's laughter from the kitchen. Life wasn't perfect. It was complicated, and there were still unhealed wounds between them. But right now, in this quiet space, there was understanding, forgiveness, and something they hadn't had in years—hope for what might come next.

Mark's voice dropped to a hushed tone, as if sharing a secret kept close to his heart. "You know, years ago, I thought letting you go was the right way to protect you. I thought it would spare us both pain. Looking back... it was fear, not love, that made me walk away. I realize now that real love doesn't run from the hard things. It faces them."

Chapter 15

The parsonage lay quiet, save for the soft tick of the mantel clock and the muffled sound of wind rustling against the windows. Emma sat curled into the corner of the couch, her knees tucked up to her chest and a throw blanket draped over her lap. It was quiet—maybe too quiet, considering the storm of thoughts swirling in her mind.

Her journal sat untouched beside her, her favorite pen resting on top of it, but she hadn't yet gathered the courage to open it. Not tonight. There was too much weight pressing down on her chest, too many emotions tangled up inside her. The conversation at Mark's house kept replaying in her head, like an old film reel she couldn't stop watching—his apology, the admission of fear. It had all been too much, too raw, too... real. Yet she needed to hear it.

She glanced out the window, where the snow had started falling again, tiny flurries floating softly against the dim glow of the porch lights. Christmas lights blinked from the houses down the road, their colors dancing across the snow like a delicate kaleidoscope. Normally, a scene like this would have brought Emma peace—the quiet beauty of winter in Laurel Ridge. But tonight, her heart was restless.

Mark's face haunted her. The way his voice had cracked when he spoke about his regrets, about Maggie. His vulnerability was something she hadn't expected. She had gotten so used to viewing him as the man who had walked away that hearing his pain—every bit as real as her own—left her off balance.

What if they tried again? Could things really be different? Could she risk her heart, knowing how easily it could break all over again?

The front door creaked open, pulling Emma out of her thoughts. She turned her head as Andrew stepped in.

"Hey, I didn't think you'd still be up," Andrew said, kicking off his snow-dusted boots by the entryway.

Emma gave a soft smile that didn't quite reach her eyes. "Just sitting here lost in thought," she murmured, pulling the blanket tighter around her shoulders.

Andrew paused. His big-brother instincts were sharp at picking up on shifts in her mood. He narrowed his eyes, studying her for a moment before making his way into the living room. "You've got that look," he said as he dropped down onto the armchair across from her. "The one where you're trying to figure out the meaning of life. Care to share what's on your mind?"

Emma pressed her lips together, unsure at first. Talking about Mark had always been a tricky thing between the two of them. Andrew loved Mark like a brother, but she was his actual sister, and those loyalties didn't always line up so perfectly. Still, Emma trusted him. More than anyone. And if there was one thing she had learned over the years, it was that keeping things bottled up never made them easier to carry.

She sighed, letting her shoulders relax just enough to let the words out. "It's Mark."

Andrew's brows lifted. He leaned back in his chair, folding his arms loosely over his chest. A spark of curiosity played in his hazel eyes. "Ah. So, that's what's got you all knotted up."

Emma nodded. "We talked tonight. Really talked." The emotions in her chest fluttered weakly as she admitted it.

Andrew said nothing at first, letting the moment hang suspended between them. He wasn't the kind of brother who rushed to fill a void in conversation; he had always known when to just listen.

Emma took a deep breath and let it spill. "He apologized, Andrew. For... everything. About walking away all those years ago, and about why he did it. He said he was scared—scared I had all these plans for my future and that he didn't fit into them. And then he also talked about Maggie, about losing her."

Andrew's face softened, and he tilted his head slightly. "I see. That's a lot to take in."

"Yeah." Emma swallowed, her throat feeling tighter than before. "It... It shook me, hearing his side. I guess I spent so much time being hurt by it that I never fully stopped and tried to consider things from his side, or figure out in my head why he left the way he did. All these years, I thought it was me, or maybe he found someone new because I wasn't good enough."

Andrew nodded, studying her carefully. "And hearing the truth tonight... did it change things for you?"

The question hung in the air like a challenge to her heart. In many ways, it had changed everything. Mark's words had opened up old wounds, yes, but they had also started to heal them in ways she didn't think could happen.

"Maybe," she admitted, her voice barely a whisper. "Part of me wants to forgive him, but I'm... I'm scared, Andrew. What if I open up again, and it just falls apart like before? Losing him once was hard enough. Yet, I know forgiveness is the right thing to do...but Andrew... he acted like such a jerk back then, and he really hurt me..."

She trailed off, her hands twisting the edges of the blanket as her thoughts overwhelmed her, the words coming in a rush. "What if losing him again is more than I can handle?"

Andrew frowned, his brow furrowed as he processed what she was saying. Then he leaned forward slightly in his chair, resting his elbows on his knees, his gaze intent.

"You've been through a lot, Em," he said gently, his voice full of brotherly affection. "More than most people handle in a lifetime. But you're still here. You made it through losing Mark the first time. You made it through Rhett's loss. Furthermore, you're still standing. And here you are back at home where you belong, ready for a fresh start. And now Mark has stepped back into your life. He apologized for his actions. Those are the facts."

He paused, letting that settle before continuing, his tone thoughtful. "Do you think this is all just a coincidence? That after all these years, both of you have been brought back together... whether it be as friends or something more for no reason?"

Emma blinked, staring at him for a moment.

"I don't know," she whispered, shaking her head. "I don't want to make the wrong choice. What if God's telling me to hold back, to protect myself?"

Andrew tilted his head, his gentle laughter warm but wise. "Or what if He's telling you to trust Him? To step out in faith, knowing that yes, there are unknowns, but those are precisely the places where God's grace shows up the strongest?"

Emma's eyes dropped back to her lap, where her fingers dug into the material of the blanket. "It's just... I'm not sure my heart can handle more loss," she admitted. "I'm moving forward after Rhett, because I have to. It's the right thing to do for me. But throwing myself into love again—into Mark—feels like I'm setting myself up. And that terrifies me."

Andrew didn't rush to answer. The house around them fell back into silence. The only sound was the slight crackle of the December wind pressing itself against the parsonage. Finally, he sat back and tugged one hand through his dark hair.

"Mark's scared too, Emma," Andrew said earnestly, his expression soft. "I know that because we talk... and if I'm being honest with you? Seeing both you and Mark go through the pain you've been through, neither of you coming out unscathed... well, it reminds me of something Grandpa used to say."

Emma lifted her gaze to meet his, curious despite the weight pressing down on her soul. "What's that?"

Andrew gave a small, knowing nod as he smiled softly, rubbing his chin. "The strongest hearts are the ones most capable of love, but also the ones that have been tested the hardest."

Emma chuckled despite herself, smiling softly at the memory of their grandfather. "He was full of those little sayings, wasn't he?"

"Yeah, he was," Andrew acknowledged with a grin. "But here's the thing—God doesn't call us to live in fear of heartbreak. He calls us to live in trust that His love is greater than whatever pain we've gone through."

Emma exhaled slowly, the knot in her heart loosening just a little at Andrew's words. But she still struggled to grasp what that meant for her in the here and now. Her heart had been bruised one too many times, and it was hard to imagine opening it all the way again.

"But what about the risk of losing again?" Emma murmured. "Isn't it safer just to... I don't know, guard my heart? Stay... stay closed off?"

Andrew's smile was compassionate. "I think that's the thing about love. It asks us to trust, even when it doesn't make sense. To believe, even when it feels like the odds aren't in our favor. And honestly, Emma... I think God is giving you and Mark this chance for a reason. If you're willing to take it. But you have to decide if you're ready to step past the fear of the unknown and trust that maybe love is worth the risk."

Emma huffed a quiet laugh, her emotions spinning in circles. "Andrew, you and your pastoral wisdom," she teased lightly.

"Comes in handy sometimes, huh?" Andrew's grin widened as he sat back with a bright glint of humor in his eyes. Then his voice softened again. "But seriously, sis... You have to wrestle with this one. I know that. But I don't think loving Mark again has to be about expecting it to end in loss. It doesn't have to be a repeat of the past, Emma. Maybe it's about giving grace to both of you for the ways you've grown through your trials and trusting that God's right there with you."

Emma sat with his words for a moment longer, letting them sink in deeply. Trust. Grace. Love without guarantees.

Could she really open her heart all the way again? Could she trust that even if things didn't go perfectly, God's hand would be there, holding her through it?

"I'll leave you to think," Andrew finally said, standing up from his chair and giving her shoulder a gentle squeeze as he walked past. "But whatever you decide, Emma? I'll back you up. Always."

Emma smiled, watching as her brother padded towards the kitchen. It was good to hear his voice, to feel the calm that came when big-brother wisdom stepped in like always. But she still had to face the questions that had tied her heart in knots all evening.

What would complete forgiveness look like? Was she strong enough to try again?

The wind rose outside, howling softly against the windows as Emma leaned back in her seat, staring at the Christmas tree lights twinkling nearby. They cast soft, shimmering patterns across the room, reminding her of the simpler, easier days of her childhood—when Christmas was all about the tree, and cookies, and time spent with family. Back then, love had felt pure, uncomplicated.

But it wasn't as simple anymore. Time had changed things. People got hurt. Trust got shattered. Hearts got broken. And somehow... life went on.

A lump formed in her throat as she thought about Mark again, about the years that had stretched between them, the unspoken hurts, the unhealed wounds. But through it all, Mark had changed—he wasn't the same impulsive guy who had broken her heart. He was a man now—a father who adored his daughter, a man who had been through his own share of loss.

Wasn't that worth considering?

Chapter 16

The winter morning sun filtered through Emma's office window, as she stood on tiptoe, stretching to hang a string of twinkling lights along the wall. Christmas music played quietly from her phone—Silent Night drifting through the air as she worked, humming along while transforming her office into a cozy holiday haven.

She'd arrived early, determined to add some festive cheer to the sterile space. Now, scattered across her desk, were the decorations she'd found in one of her boxes stored in Andrew's garage—a small artificial tree, some battery-operated candles, and a few carefully chosen ornaments that spoke to both the season and her faith.

As she decorated, Emma's thoughts drifted to this past weekend—to warm moments in Mark's kitchen, decorating cookies with Olivia, and that deep conversation that had followed. Her hands stilled as she remembered the vulnerability in Mark's voice when he'd apologized.

The weekend had shifted something between them—something she couldn't quite name but felt in every quiet moment since. It was as if their honest conversation had cleared away years of uncertainty, leaving room for... what exactly? Emma wasn't sure, but her heart felt lighter, more open to possibilities.

Shaking herself from her reverie, Emma returned to her decorating. She'd just finished arranging a collection of paper snowflakes made by some of the students when a knock echoed through the room. She turned to find Mark leaning against her door frame, a warm smile playing at the corners of his mouth.

"Looks like someone's been busy," he said, his eyes scanning the transformed space with appreciation.

"Just trying to make things a bit more cheerful. You know how intimidating a nurse's office can be for kids."

Mark stepped into the room, his gaze taking in the twinkling lights and festive touches. "Well, I'd say you've succeeded. This definitely doesn't feel like a typical school nurse's office anymore."

"That's the idea," Emma replied, adjusting a snowflake that hung slightly crooked. "Though I have to admit, some of these decorations might be more for me than the students. I've always loved making spaces feel cozy and festive during Christmas."

Mark's eyes crinkled at the corners as he smiled. "I remember. You used to go all out decorating your locker in high school. What was it you called it? Your 'winter wonderland in miniature'?"

Emma laughed, surprised. "I can't believe you remember that! Yes, and as I recall, you teased me mercilessly about it."

"Only because it made you blush," Mark admitted, his voice carrying a hint of playfulness that made Emma's heart flutter. He moved closer, examining the nativity scene on the windowsill. "This is beautiful," he said, his finger gently touching the edge of the display. "It reminds me of the one my mom puts out every year."

Emma nodded, watching as he studied the careful arrangement. "It was my grandmother's. She gave it to me before she passed, said it would help me remember what Christmas is really about, even when life gets overwhelming."

Mark turned to face her, his expression thoughtful. "She was a wise woman." He paused, seeming to gather his thoughts before speaking again. "Speaking of Christmas... Olivia and I were planning to head to the Christmas tree farm after school today. She's been asking—well, more like insisting, really—that you join us."

Emma's heart skipped a beat at the invitation, but she tried to keep her voice steady. "Has she now?"

Mark's smile widened. "Oh yes. She's quite determined. And," he added, his voice softening, "I have to admit, I'm hoping you will come with us. It's always more fun with good company."

"I'd love to. It's been years since I've picked out a real Christmas tree," she said.

"Perfect," Mark said, his entire face lighting up with genuine pleasure. "We can meet in the parking lot after the last bell? Olivia will be thrilled."

The morning bell rang, signaling the start of classes. Mark straightened, adjusting his tie. "Well, duty calls. But I'll see you later?"

Emma nodded, trying to ignore the way her pulse quickened at his smile. "Later," she agreed.

He paused in the doorway, turning back with that gentle grin that seemed reserved just for her. "Oh, and Emma? The office looks wonderful. It feels like a winter wonderland."

As Mark disappeared down the hallway, Emma stood in the middle of her newly decorated office, her heart beating a little faster than usual. She glanced around at the twinkling lights and festive decorations, everything somehow looking brighter than it had moments before.

"What are you doing, Emma?" she whispered to herself, but she couldn't stop the smile that spread across her face. The rest of the school day stretched ahead, but suddenly, all she could think about was the promise of picking out a Christmas tree with Mark and Olivia.

***

The afternoon seemed to crawl by at a snail's pace. Emma tended to the usual parade of students—bandaging scraped knees, checking temperatures, and offering gentle reassurance to those who just needed a quiet moment away from class. But her mind kept drifting to the evening ahead, to the prospect of Christmas tree hunting with Mark and Olivia.

When the last bell of the school day rang, Emma gathered her things with barely contained excitement. She pulled on her warm winter coat, wrapped a soft blue scarf around her neck, and grabbed her purse. After one last glance around her festive office, she switched off the lights and headed toward the parking lot.

The cold air bit at her cheeks as she stepped outside, but the discomfort faded when she spotted Mark and Olivia waiting by his truck. Olivia, bouncing on her toes with characteristic enthusiasm, caught sight of Emma first.

"Miss Emma!" Olivia called out, waving frantically. "You're really coming with us! Daddy said you would, but I wanted to make sure!"

Emma laughed, the sound carrying across the crisp winter air. "Of course! I wouldn't miss picking out a Christmas tree with my favorite student."

"I'm your favorite?" Olivia beamed, her face lighting up like a Christmas tree.

"Don't let the other kids hear that," Mark stage-whispered, winking at Emma over Olivia's head. "We'll have a riot on our hands."

Emma reached them, and Olivia immediately attached herself to Emma's side. "Will you ride in the back seat with me, Miss Emma? Please?"

Mark shook his head, amused. "Actually, Liv, Miss Emma probably wants to follow in her own car. That way, she can head home afterward without having to come all the way back here."

Emma found herself oddly disappointed by the practical suggestion, though she knew it made sense. "He's right, sweetie. But I'll be right behind you the whole way.

"Promise you won't get lost?" Olivia asked, her brown eyes serious.

"I promise," Emma assured her, then glanced at Mark. "Though it has been a while since I've been to the Christmas tree farm. It's still out on Old Mill Road, right?"

Mark nodded. "Same place it's always been. Just follow us—I'll drive slow enough that you won't lose sight of us."

They separated to their respective vehicles, and Emma couldn't help but smile at Olivia's dramatic wave goodbye, as if they weren't going to see each other again in just a few minutes.

The drive to the Christmas tree farm was peaceful, with Mark's red pickup leading the way through the winding mountain roads of Laurel Ridge. The late afternoon sun cast long shadows across the snow-covered landscape, and Emma thought about past Christmases—of family traditions and the simple joy of selecting the perfect tree.

When they pulled into the Christmas tree farm's gravel parking lot, Emma's breath caught at the magical scene before her. Rows upon rows of evergreens stretched into the distance, their branches dusted with fresh snow. Strings of white lights crisscrossed overhead, creating a canopy of twinkling stars, even though the sun hadn't set yet. The scent of evergreen and wood smoke filled the air, mixing with the sweet aroma of hot chocolate wafting from the small cabin that served as the farm's shop.

Emma had barely stepped out of her car when Olivia bounded over, practically vibrating with excitement. "Come on, Miss Emma! We have to find the perfect tree before it gets dark!"

"Hold on there, sweetheart," Mark called out, coming around his truck to join them. "We need to get a sled first to pull the tree on, and don't forget what happened last year when you ran ahead."

Olivia's face scrunched up in remembrance. "I got lost in the big trees," she admitted sheepishly to Emma. "Daddy had to come find me."

"Scared me half to death," Mark added, though his tone was gentle. "So this year, we stick together, right?"

"Right!" Olivia agreed, reaching for both Mark's and Emma's hands. "We can all find the perfect tree together!

Emma's heart melted at the natural way Olivia included her, as if she had always been part of their Christmas tradition. She caught Mark's eye and saw her own emotion reflected there.

They made their way to the small cabin first, where a cheerful elderly man with rosy cheeks handed them a sled. "Welcome back, Thompson family!" he said, then noticed Emma. His eyes twinkled as he glanced between her and Mark. "And who might this lovely addition be?"

"This is Miss Emma!" Olivia announced proudly before either adult could speak. She's my school nurse, and she's helping us pick out our tree!"

"Well, isn't that nice," the man said, his smile growing wider. "I'm Harold. Been running this tree farm longer than these two have been alive," he added with a wink toward Emma. "And I must say, it does my heart good to see folks coming together for Christmas."

Emma felt her cheeks warm at the implication, but before she could correct his assumption, Olivia was tugging them outside toward the rows of trees, her excitement impossible to contain.

"Remember," Mark called out as they followed Olivia's lead, "we need something that will fit in the living room. No ten-footers this year!"

"I know, Daddy," Olivia sighed with the patience of someone who had heard this reminder many times. "But it has to be perfect!"

They weaved through the rows of trees, Olivia inspecting each one with serious concentration. The late afternoon sun filtered through the branches, casting dappled shadows on the snow beneath their feet. Emma noticed how the golden light caught in Mark's hair, highlighting the touches of gray at his temples.

"What about this one?" Olivia called out, stopping in front of a full, symmetrical tree that stood about seven feet tall.

Mark circled the tree, checking its shape from all angles. "It's a beautiful tree, peanut, but look at the top—it's leaning to the left. The star would be crooked."

Olivia's face fell slightly, but she squared her shoulders and moved on to the next candidate. As they walked, Mark fell into step beside Emma, their shoulders occasionally brushing in a way that sent tiny sparks through her.

"She takes this very seriously," Emma observed with a smile.

Mark chuckled. "Oh, you have no idea. Last year, we looked at every single tree on the farm before she made her decision. I thought we'd be here until New Year's."

"How long did it actually take?"

"Two hours," he said with a dramatic groan that made Emma laugh. "Though I have to admit, she did pick out a beautiful tree in the end."

They continued their search, with Olivia leading the way and occasionally calling them over to inspect particularly promising candidates. The air grew colder as the sun sank lower in the sky, but the strands of lights overhead began to twinkle more brightly, creating a magical atmosphere.

"Miss Emma!" Olivia's excited voice rang out. "I found it! I really found it this time!"

They made their way to where Olivia stood, bouncing with anticipation. The tree before them was slightly shorter than the others they'd looked at, and one side had a small bare patch where the branches hadn't filled in completely. But there was something charming about it—a certain character in its imperfection.

"Sweetheart," Mark began gently, "are you sure? This one's a bit... different from what you usually pick."

"I know," Olivia said, her voice serious. "But look—it's special. See how it's shaped like a heart on this side?" She pointed to where the branches naturally formed a heart-like pattern. "Remember what you always say about how God loves us, even when we're not perfect?"

Mark's expression softened, and Emma felt her own heart twist at the pure wisdom in Olivia's words. "You're right," Mark said, crouching down to Olivia's level. "Sometimes the most beautiful things are the ones that might seem a little different at first glance."

His eyes flickered to Emma's for just a moment, and she felt the weight of unspoken meaning in his gaze. Her hand unconsciously moved to touch the scar on her neck—her own imperfection that she usually tried to hide.

"I think it's perfect," Emma said, stepping closer to the tree.

Olivia beamed up at her. "Yeah! Can we get this one, Daddy? Please?"

Mark stood, brushing snow from his knees. "Yes, this is definitely our tree."

As Mark cut the tree, Emma and Olivia stood back, watching. The little girl slipped her hand into Emma's, leaning against her side.

"Miss Emma?" Olivia asked quietly.

"Yes, sweetie?"

"I'm really glad you came with us today. It makes it even more special."

Emma squeezed Olivia's hand gently, trying to swallow past the sudden lump in her throat. "I'm really glad I came too."

Mark made quick work of cutting down the tree, his movements sure and practiced. As he and Emma worked together to secure it to the sled, their hands brushed several times, sending little jolts of awareness through Emma's body. She noticed how Mark's touch lingered just a fraction longer than necessary when he helped steady her on the snowy ground, his hand warm and strong against her elbow.

"Everything okay?" he asked, noticing her slight shiver.

"Just a little cold," Emma replied, though the warmth in her cheeks had nothing to do with the temperature.

"We should head back to the cabin," Mark suggested, his voice carrying a note of concern. "They usually have hot chocolate, and I think someone," he glanced meaningfully at Olivia, who was trying to make snow angels nearby, "could use a warm-up."

They made their way back toward the cabin, drawing their precious cargo behind them. The sun had nearly set now, and the strands of lights overhead cast a magical atmosphere across the snowy landscape.

The small cabin had transformed in the growing darkness, its windows now sparkled with twinkling Christmas lights and the flicker of a fire within. As they approached the door, Olivia suddenly stopped in her tracks, pointing upward with a delighted gasp.

"Look! Mistletoe!"

Emma's heart skipped a beat as she followed Olivia's gesture to the small sprig of greenery hanging from the cabin's entrance. Mark had stopped too.

"Daddy, you and Miss Emma have to kiss!" Olivia announced with all the innocent enthusiasm of a seven-year-old. "That's the rule!"

Emma felt her face flame as Mark cleared his throat. "Sweetie, I don't think—"

"But it's tradition!" Olivia insisted, her bottom lip starting to quiver just slightly.

Mark met Emma's eyes, his expression a mix of embarrassment and something else—something that made her pulse quicken. "We can probably skip the tradition just this once," he said softly, though his gaze lingered on Emma's face a moment longer than necessary.

"He's right," Emma managed to say, trying to sound casual despite her racing heart. "Sometimes traditions can wait for the right moment."

Olivia looked between them, clearly disappointed but willing to accept their decision. "Okay," she sighed dramatically. "But maybe next time?"

"How about some hot chocolate instead?" Mark suggested quickly, steering them away from the mistletoe and into the cabin.

The warmth inside enveloped them at once, along with the rich scent of cocoa and cinnamon. Harold greeted them cheerfully from behind the counter, where he was arranging a display of handmade ornaments.

"Found the perfect tree, I see!" he called out. "Hot chocolate's fresh—on the house for my favorite customers."

While Mark went to settle the bill for the tree, Emma and Olivia explored the cabin's small gift shop. The walls were lined with holiday decorations, most of them handcrafted by local artisans. One display in particular caught Emma's eye—a collection of wooden ornaments, each one intricately carved with different winter scenes.

"These are beautiful," she murmured, picking up one that depicted a small church in the snow, remarkably similar to the one in Laurel Ridge.

"They're all made by my grandson," Harold said, coming up beside her. "He has quite a gift, doesn't he?"

Emma nodded, turning the ornament over in her hands. The detail was extraordinary—she could almost hear the church bells ringing across the snow-covered square.

"That one's special," Harold continued, his voice softening. "It's based on our own little church in town.

Emma's fingers stilled on the ornament as memories washed over her—of youth group meetings, of stolen glances across the church pew, of a young Mark Thompson helping her mother carry Christmas decorations up the church steps.

"Emma?" Mark's voice brought her back to the present. He had finished paying and now stood beside her, three cups of hot chocolate in his hands. His eyes fell on the ornament she held. "That's beautiful."

"Isn't it?" she said softly, moving to return it to the display.

But Mark stopped her with a gentle touch to her wrist. "Wait," he said, then turned to Harold. "We'll take this ornament too, please."

"Mark, you don't have to—"

I want to," he said, his eyes meeting hers with an intensity that made her breath catch. "Consider it a welcome home gift."

Harold wrapped the ornament carefully in tissue paper, his knowing smile making Emma's cheeks warm again. As he handed her the small package, she could have sworn she heard him whisper, "Some traditions are worth waiting for."

Outside, the snow had started falling again, fat flakes drifting lazily through the illuminated night air. Olivia walked ahead to the truck, her own hot chocolate clutched carefully in her mitten'd hands.

"Thank you," Emma said, holding the wrapped ornament close. "For this, and... for today. It was wonderful."

Mark's smile was warm enough to melt the surrounding snow. "Thank you for coming. It made finding a Christmas tree even more special."

"Miss Emma!" Olivia's voice rang out with childlike enthusiasm. "Will you come home with daddy and I and help us decorate the Christmas Tree?"

Chapter 17

Emma hesitated, her hand still wrapped around the delicate package holding the church ornament. She glanced at Mark, searching his face for any sign of reluctance at Olivia's impromptu invitation.

Instead, she found affection in his eyes as he said, "That's a great idea, Olivia. What do you say, Emma? Want to help us give this special tree a proper welcome home?"

The invitation hung in the air between them, weighted with possibility. Emma knew she should probably head home—it was getting late, and she had work tomorrow. But something about the way Mark looked at her, and the way Olivia bounced on her toes in anticipation, made all her practical reasons fade away like snowflakes on warm skin.

"I'd love to," she said, and Olivia's squeal of delight echoed across the snowy parking lot.

"You can follow us back." Mark said, his smile softening the corners of his eyes. "We'll take it slow—the roads might be getting slippery."

Snow continued to fall in large, lazy flakes, catching in the beam of her headlights as she followed Mark's truck through the quiet, curvy mountain roads surrounding Laurel Ridge.

When they arrived at Mark's house, the porch lights cast a welcoming light across the fresh snow. Olivia got out of the truck, her excitement seemingly multiplied now that they were home.

"Careful on the steps." Mark called out as she rushed toward the house. "They might be slippery!" He turned to Emma with an apologetic smile. "She never slows down—pure Christmas energy this time of year."

Emma laughed. "It's adorable. She reminds me of myself at that age—I used to drive my parents crazy with my Christmas enthusiasm."

Together, they worked to get the tree out of the bed of the truck and into the house, their breath coming out in visible puffs in the cold air. Mark's hands were steady and sure as he guided the tree through the front door, and Emma couldn't help but notice how the muscles in his arms flexed beneath his coat.

Olivia had already shed her coat and boots and was busy dragging boxes of Christmas decorations away from a nearby corner of the living room.

"I got the boxes moved, Daddy!" she announced proudly, dragging a large container marked 'CHRISTMAS' across the floor.

"Hold on there, sweetheart," Mark chuckled. "Let's get the tree in the stand first. Why don't you help Miss Emma with her coat while I set this up?"

Olivia immediately abandoned her box-moving mission and bounded over to Emma. "I can hang up your coat right here," she said, pointing to a wooden peg by the door.

Emma smiled. As she handed Olivia her coat, she caught Mark's eye across the room. He was watching them with an expression that made her heart flutter.

The next hour passed in a blur of Christmas magic. Mark got the tree secured in its stand while Emma and Olivia carefully unpacked ornaments, each one seeming to hold its own story. Olivia proudly showed Emma her favorites, including a small angel she'd made in Sunday school and a glittery pine cone that had been her mother's.

"This one was Mommy's favorite," Olivia said softly, holding up a delicate glass ball with hand-painted snowflakes. "Daddy lets me hang it every year, but I have to be extra careful.

Emma glanced at Mark, who had stilled in his work of untangling the Christmas lights. His expression held a mixture of love and melancholy that caused Emma's heartache.

"I bet your mom would be so proud of how carefully you handle her special ornament," Emma said, and Olivia's face lit up with a bright smile.

"Do you think so?"

"I know so," Emma assured her, helping her find the perfect spot for the precious ornament.

Mark finished with the lights, and soon the tree was transformed into a twinkling wonderland. They worked together, passing ornaments back and forth, their hands occasionally brushing in ways that sent little thrills through Emma. Olivia flitted between them, directing their placement with all the authority of a tiny Christmas decorator.

"Miss Emma," Olivia said suddenly, "where should we put your new ornament? The one with the church?"

Emma had almost forgotten about the carved wooden ornament Mark had bought her. She looked up at Mark and said, "I left it in my vehicle. Do you want the ornament on your tree?"

"I'll be right back," Mark said with a warm smile. He slipped on his boots and headed out into the crisp night air.

When he returned, snow dusting his shoulders, he held the small ornament wrapped in delicate tissue paper. Emma carefully unwrapped it. The carved scene of Laurel Ridge's church seemed to come alive in the glow of the Christmas lights, each intricate detail catching and reflecting the warm illumination.

"I think..." She looked at the tree thoughtfully, then pointed to a spot near the heart-shaped gap in the branches. "Right here. What do you think?"

Olivia nodded enthusiastically. "It's perfect! Right next to the heart because church is all about love, right Daddy?"

Mark moved closer, his presence warm at Emma's side. "That's right, Liv. And sometimes... sometimes love finds its way back to where it began."

Emma's breath caught at his words, at the way his voice had softened when he said them. She hung the ornament carefully, its wooden surface smooth beneath her fingers.

"There," she said, stepping back to admire their work. "Now it's perfect."

The tree was beautiful, its imperfections only adding to its charm. The bare patch seemed to frame the ornaments perfectly, creating a unique display that couldn't have been planned better.

"You know what we need now?" Olivia announced, bouncing on her toes. "Hot chocolate! With marshmallows!"

Mark laughed. "More hot chocolate?"

"Please?" Olivia batted her eyes dramatically. "It's tradition, Daddy! And Miss Emma needs to try your special recipe!"

"Special recipe?" Emma raised an eyebrow, intrigued.

Mark rubbed the back of his neck, a slight flush creeping up his cheeks. "It's nothing fancy—just something I came up with that Olivia seems to think is magic."

"It is magic!" Olivia insisted. "Please make it, Daddy? For Miss Emma?"

Mark's "magic" hot chocolate turned out to be a production worthy of its reputation. Emma watched from her perch at the kitchen island as he moved with practiced ease, gathering ingredients: rich chocolate, whole milk, a hint of vanilla, and what he claimed was his "secret ingredient"—though Emma caught a glimpse of cinnamon being added when he thought she wasn't looking.

Olivia sat beside Emma, swinging her legs and chattering happily about their tree-decorating success. "And did you see how pretty the lights look when they twinkle? Daddy always says the lights remind him of stars, and stars remind us of the Christmas star that led people to baby Jesus."

Emma smiled, warmth spreading through her chest at Olivia's innocent wisdom. "That's a beautiful way to think about it," she agreed, watching as Mark stirred the hot chocolate on the stove.

The kitchen filled with the rich aroma of chocolate and spices, mixing with the scent of evergreen from their freshly decorated tree.

"Here we go." Mark announced, carrying three steaming mugs. Each one was topped with a generous helping of whipped cream and a light dusting of what looked like cocoa powder and cinnamon.

"Ta-da!" Olivia exclaimed, clapping her hands. "Isn't it pretty, Miss Emma? Daddy makes it look like art!"

Emma had to admit, the presentation was impressive. She wrapped her hands around the warm mug, breathing in the heavenly aroma. "It smells amazing."

"Wait till you taste it," Mark said, his eyes crinkling at the corners as he watched her take her first sip.

The hot chocolate was unlike anything Emma had ever tasted—rich and velvety, with layers of flavor that seemed to unfold on her tongue. The hint of cinnamon added warmth without overpowering the chocolate, and something else—something she couldn't quite name—gave it an almost magical quality.

"Oh my goodness," she breathed, looking up to find Mark watching her with a pleased expression. "This really is special."

"Told you!" Olivia said triumphantly, her own whipped cream mustache making her look absolutely adorable. "It's the best hot chocolate in the whole world!"

Mark chuckled, reaching over to wipe a spot of whipped cream from Olivia's nose with a napkin. "I wouldn't go that far."

"No, she's right," Emma said, taking another appreciative sip. "This is incredible. You'll have to teach me your secret recipe someday."

The words slipped out before she could stop them, carrying more weight than she'd intended. They implied a future, more moments like this, more chances to share these small, precious traditions.

Mark's eyes met hers over their mugs, and something electric passed between them. "Someday," he agreed, his voice carrying a promise that made Emma's heart skip.

They sat there in comfortable silence for a moment, sipping their hot chocolate and watching the snow fall outside through the sliding glass doors. Olivia's animated chatter provided a cheerful backdrop to their quiet companionship, and Emma wished she could freeze this moment in time—preserve it like one of the precious ornaments they'd hung on the tree.

Reluctantly, Emma glanced at the clock on the wall. "I should probably head home," she said, though every part of her wanted to stay in this warm, magical bubble. "It's getting late, and we all have school tomorrow."

"No!" Olivia protested at once. "Can't you stay? Just a little longer?"

"Olivia," Mark said gently but firmly, "Miss Emma's right. It's almost your bedtime anyway, young lady."

Olivia's lower lip trembled slightly, but she nodded, sliding off her stool to give Emma a tight hug. "Thank you for helping with our tree. It's the best one ever because you helped pick it."

Emma hugged her back. "Thank you for letting me be a part of your tradition, sweetie. It means a lot to me."

Mark walked her to the door, helping her with her coat, while Olivia waved from the kitchen, still nursing the last of her hot chocolate. The porch lights cast a soft glow across the fresh snow, and Emma's breath caught at the beauty of the scene—the twinkling Christmas lights, the gentle fall of snow, the warmth of the moment.

"Drive safely," Mark said as she stepped onto the porch. "I slipped my cell phone number in the pocket of your coat. Text me when you get home?"

Emma nodded, touched by his concern. "I will." She paused, then added, "Thank you for today—for everything. The tree hunting, the ornament... it was perfect."

Mark's expression softened, and for a moment, Emma thought he might say something more. Instead, he reached out and squeezed her hand gently. "Thank you for being part of it."

As Emma drove home through the snowy night, she couldn't stop smiling. The evening played through her mind like scenes from a beloved Christmas movie—Olivia's excitement, Mark's gentle presence, the way they'd all worked together to transform a simple tree into something magical.

When she finally pulled into Andrew's driveway, she sat for a moment, watching the snow fall in the beam of her headlights. She grabbed her phone and texted Mark.

"Made it home, safe and sound. Thank you again for a wonderful evening." She typed.

His response came quickly: *"Thank you for making our tradition even more special. Sweet dreams, Emma."*

Chapter 18

The next morning dawned bright and cold, with sunlight glinting off the fresh snow that blanketed Laurel Ridge. Emma hummed quietly to herself as she organized supplies in her office, still wrapped in the happiness of the previous evening's memories.

A knock at her door interrupted her thoughts. She turned to find Wendy standing there, holding two steaming to go cups of coffee and wearing a knowing smile.

"Wendy!" Emma said with a grin. "I didn't expect to see you here. Do you always make random calls to friends while they are at work?"

"Only when I feel the need. Spill it," Wendy said, setting one of the coffees on Emma's desk. "I saw you drive by last night following Mark's truck, which, by the way, I noticed the Christmas tree he was hauling, and my gossip radar went into overdrive. What's going on there?"

Emma felt her cheeks warm as she accepted the coffee, grateful for both the caffeine and her friend's timing. Trust Wendy to show up exactly when Emma needed someone to talk to about the swirl of emotions she'd been trying to sort through.

"It's not what you think," Emma started, then paused, considering. "Or maybe it is. I'm not really sure what it is, to be honest."

Wendy settled into the chair across from Emma's desk, her eyes sparkling with interest. "Well, start at the beginning. How did you end up Christmas tree shopping with them?"

Emma took a sip of her coffee, gathering her thoughts. "Mark asked me yesterday morning if I'd like to join them. Well, technically Olivia asked, but Mark... wanted me to go too."

"Of course he did," Wendy said, as if this was the most obvious thing in the world. "Anyone with eyes can see the way he looks at you, Emma."

Emma's heart fluttered. "We talked, Wendy. Really talked this past weekend. About everything—about why he broke up with me and left all those years ago, about what happened after. It was..." she searched for the right word, "healing... and eye-opening... and he apologized."

"Finally!" Wendy exclaimed, then quickly lowered her voice, remembering they were in school. "Sorry, but you two have needed to have that conversation for years. And?"

"And it helped," Emma admitted. "Understanding why he left, hearing him apologize... it was like this weight and regret I've had for years lifted." She fiddled with her coffee cup, memories of the past few days washing over her. "Then last night, helping them pick out their tree, decorating it together... it felt so natural, so right. Like I was exactly where I was supposed to be."

Wendy leaned forward, her expression softening. "Oh, honey. You know what that means, don't you?"

Emma looked up, meeting her friend's knowing gaze. "What?"

"You're falling for him again. Or maybe you never really stopped in the first place."

The words hit Emma like a physical force, making her breath catch. Was that what this was? These feelings that had been growing stronger with each passing day, each passing year?

"It's not that simple," Emma protested. "We've both been through so much. And there's Olivia to consider…"

"Who clearly adores you," Wendy pointed out. "From what I've seen and heard around town, that little girl lights up like a Christmas tree whenever you're around."

Emma couldn't help but smile, thinking of Olivia's enthusiasm the night before, her innocent joy in sharing their traditions. "She's amazing," she admitted. "But that's part of what makes this so complicated. What if…"

"What if what?" Wendy pressed gently when Emma trailed off.

"What if I'm not ready?" Emma's voice was barely above a whisper. "What if I let myself feel all of this, let myself be part of their lives, and then something happens? After the first time with Mark and then Rhett…" She touched the scar on her neck unconsciously. "I don't know if I could survive losing someone I love again."

Wendy reached across the desk and took Emma's hand, squeezing it firmly. "First of all, you're stronger than you give yourself credit for. Second, honey, that's exactly what faith is about—trusting that God has a plan, even when we're scared. And third," her eyes twinkled, "did you just admit you love him?"

Emma's eyes widened as she realized what she'd said. "I… I didn't mean…"

"Yes, you did," Wendy said. "And that's okay. It's okay to feel scared and excited and uncertain all at the same time. But Emma, I've known you almost my whole life, and though we had a bit of a break while you were in Pittsburgh… I haven't seen you look this alive since we were teenagers. Maybe instead of focusing on all the what-ifs, you should consider that this might be exactly what you've been praying for."

Before Emma could respond, the bell rang, signaling the start of the school day. Wendy stood, gathering her empty coffee cup.

"Just think about it," she said, heading toward the door. "And remember, sometimes the best Christmas gifts are the ones we never thought to put on our wish list."

As Wendy left, Emma sat back in her chair, her friend's words echoing in her mind. She thought about Mark's smile when she'd agreed to join them last night, about the way Olivia had slipped her small hand into Emma's as they searched for the perfect tree, about the feeling of coming home she'd experienced sitting in their kitchen, drinking hot chocolate and watching the snow fall.

Maybe Wendy… and her brother… were right. Maybe it was time to stop letting fear and past hurts dictate her choices and start trusting that God had brought her back to Laurel Ridge—back to Mark—for a reason.

Her phone buzzed with a text, and her heart did a little flip when she saw Mark's name on the screen:

"Olivia insisted on showing everyone a picture on my phone of our Christmas tree at the diner this morning when we had breakfast before school. Pretty sure the whole town knows about our adventure by now. I hope that's okay."

Emma smiled, typing back: *"More than okay. It was a pretty perfect evening."*

His response came quickly: *"It really was. Thank you again for being part of it."*

As Emma set her phone down, she caught her reflection in the window—she was smiling, really smiling, in a way she hadn't in years. Maybe that was answer enough.

Chapter 19

The morning passed in a blur of Band-Aids and temperature checks, but Emma's mind kept drifting back to her conversation with Wendy. During a quiet moment between students, she thought about the church ornament Mark had bought and now hung on his Christmas tree.

Another knock at her door drew her attention. This time it was Mark, holding two paper lunch bags.

"I come asking if you'd like to join us for lunch," he said, lifting the bags slightly. "Olivia was quite insistent that I invite you to eat with us in my classroom. She packed an extra cookie in her lunch specifically to share with you."

Emma's heart melted at the gesture. "Well, I can't disappoint her then, can I?"

She gathered her own lunch, and they walked together through the busy hallways as students gathered their lunches and rushed to the lunchroom. Their shoulders brushed occasionally, sending little sparks of awareness through her body. Emma was acutely conscious of his presence beside her, of the way other teachers smiled knowingly as they passed.

Mark's fourth-grade classroom was decorated with student artwork covering the walls and a reading corner filled with comfortable cushions. Olivia was already there, having come down from her second-grade classroom.

"Miss Emma!" she exclaimed when they entered. "You came! Look, I saved you a special spot right here!" She patted the chair she'd pulled up next to her own.

Emma settled into the offered seat, watching as Olivia carefully unpacked her lunch, including the promised cookie—a slightly squashed sugar cookie with red and green sprinkles.

"I saved it just for you," Olivia said proudly, placing the cookie on a napkin for Emma. "Because you helped make our tree so special."

"Thank you, sweetie," Emma said, touched by the simple gesture of love. "That was very thoughtful of you."

"Speaking of the tree," Mark said, settling into his own chair, "Grandma and Pops are coming over for dinner tonight. They want to see our masterpiece." He paused, his eyes meeting Emma's. "You're welcome to join us if you'd like. Grandma's making her famous pot roast."

Emma's heart stuttered at the invitation. Dinner with Mark's family felt significant somehow, like crossing another threshold in whatever this was growing between them.

"Please say yes!" Olivia added enthusiastically. "Gigi makes the best biscuits ever, and maybe I can show you my favorite Christmas books after dinner!"

Mark's expression was warm as he watched his daughter's excitement, but there was something else in his eyes when he looked at Emma—a hint of vulnerability, of hope.

"I'd love to come," Emma said, and the matching smiles that spread across both Mark and Olivia's faces made her heart flip.

"Excellent," Mark said. "Dinner's at six."

The rest of lunch passed in a comfortable flow of conversation, with Olivia dominating most of it as she told Emma about her morning in Mrs. Davis's class and her excitement about the upcoming church Christmas play rehearsal.

As they were cleaning up, Olivia suddenly gasped. "Daddy! We forgot to tell Miss Emma about the Christmas festival!"

"Ah, that's right," Mark said, gathering their lunch containers. "The town's annual Winter Festival is this Saturday. There's ice skating, holiday vendors, the lighting of the town Christmas tree..."

"And hot chocolate and cookies and Christmas carols and—" Olivia's enthusiasm bubbled over.

"And," Mark cut in gently, his eyes meeting Emma's, "I was wondering if you'd like to go with us? As a... proper date?"

The word 'date' hung in the air between them, charged with meaning. Emma's breath caught as she processed what he was asking. This wasn't just a casual invitation to join them at a community event—this was Mark explicitly acknowledging that something was shifting between them, something worth exploring.

Olivia looked between them, her eyes wide with hope, while Mark waited patiently for Emma's response, his expression a mix of nervousness and quiet determination.

Emma's heart thundered in her chest as she looked at Mark, seeing both the boy she'd loved years ago and the man he'd become—strong and steady, and brave enough to take this step. Her gaze flickered to Olivia, who was practically vibrating with anticipation, and then back to Mark.

"I'd love to," she said.

"Really?" Olivia squealed, jumping up and down. "This is going to be the best festival ever!"

The first bell signaling the end of lunch period rang, and Olivia quickly gathered her things. "I gotta go. I'll see you at dinner, right, Miss Emma?"

"Right," Emma confirmed, watching as Olivia practically skipped out of the room, her joy infectious.

Once they were alone, Mark moved closer to Emma, his voice low and warm. "Thank you. For saying yes. To dinner tonight and to the festival."

"Thank you for asking," Emma replied, very aware of how close he was standing. "Though I have to warn you, I'm a terrible ice skater."

Mark's eyes crinkled at the corners as he smiled. "Don't worry. I won't let you fall."

The promise in his words seemed to encompass more than just ice skating, and Emma felt her cheeks warm. Before she could respond, students began filtering into the classroom for the afternoon session.

"See you tonight?" Mark asked, taking a small step back.

Emma nodded. "Tonight," she confirmed, and the way Mark's eyes lingered on her as she left the classroom made her feel like she was floating all the way back to her office.

The afternoon seemed to crawl by yet again, but finally, the last bell rang. Emma gathered her things and as she was about to leave, her phone buzzed with a text from Mark:

"Looking forward to dinner. Don't forget to bring your appetite—Grandma always makes enough food to feed an army."

Emma smiled, typing back: *"Can't wait. Should I bring anything?"*

His response came quickly: *"Just yourself. That's more than enough."*

As Emma drove home, she found herself humming Christmas carols, her heart light. She thought about Mark asking her on a proper date, about Olivia's enthusiasm, about the way everything seemed to be falling into place like pieces of a puzzle.

Maybe Wendy was right. Maybe instead of worrying about all the what-ifs, she should focus on the gift God seemed to be offering her—a second chance at love, at family, at building something beautiful from the broken pieces of her past.

Chapter 20

Emma pulled into Mark's driveway precisely at six, her heart doing a little dance as she spotted the twinkling lights on the Christmas tree through the windows.

She'd changed into a soft cream sweater and dark jeans, and she'd let her hair fall in natural waves around her shoulders. The night air was crisp and cold as she made her way up the porch steps, carrying a small gift bag.

Before she could knock, the door flew open, revealing an excited Olivia. "Miss Emma! You're here!" She was still in her school clothes but had added a festive red ribbon to her hair.

"Olivia," came Mark's voice from inside, "what have I said about opening the door without checking first?"

"But I knew it was Miss Emma," Olivia protested, grabbing Emma's hand and pulling her inside. "I was watching from the window!"

The house smelled amazing—a mix of pot roast, freshly baked bread, and something sweetly spiced that made Emma's mouth water.

Mark appeared from the kitchen, wiping his hands on a dish towel. He'd changed too, wearing a forest green button-down shirt that brought out the warmth in his eyes.

"Hi," he said softly, his gaze traveling over her in a way that made her cheeks warm.

"Hi," she replied, suddenly feeling shy despite the comfortable familiarity they'd developed.

"You shouldn't have brought anything," Mark said, noticing the gift bag in her hand.

Emma smiled. "This isn't for dinner. It's actually for Olivia."

"For me?" Olivia's eyes widened with delight.

"You mentioned favorite Christmas books earlier today," Emma explained, holding out the bag. "And I remembered having this one when I was your age. I thought you might like it, too."

Olivia carefully pulled out a beautifully illustrated copy of "The Night Before Christmas," her face lighting up as she opened it to reveal the magical pictures inside.

"Look, Daddy!" she exclaimed. "The pictures are so pretty! Can we read it tonight? Please?"

"After dinner," Mark promised, his eyes meeting Emma's with a warmth that made her heart flutter. "Thank you," he added softly. "That was very thoughtful."

"Well, well, look who's here!" Clair's voice rang out as she appeared from the kitchen, wearing an apron and a knowing smile. "Emma, dear, you look lovely."

She pulled Emma into a warm hug that smelled like home-baked biscuits and felt like a mother's love. "I'm so glad you could join us tonight. Eli's just building up the fire—why don't you all go get settled in the living room while I finish up in the kitchen?"

"Can I help with anything?" Emma offered, but Clair waved her off.

"Not tonight, dear. Tonight, you're our guest. Though I might take you up on that offer another time, she added with a wink that made Emma's heart warm at the implication of future family dinners.

"Come on, Miss Emma!" Olivia grabbed her hand again. "I want to show you how pretty the tree looks again!"

They moved into the living room, where Eli was indeed tending to a crackling fire. He looked up as they entered, his face creasing into a warm smile.

"Emma," he greeted, standing to give her a gentle hug. "It's good to see you again. The house feels brighter with you in it."

Emma felt tears prick her eyes at the simple welcome, at how easily they all included her in their family circle. She caught Mark watching her, his expression soft and full of something that made her pause for a moment.

The tree they'd decorated the night before stood in the corner, its lights twinkling magically. The bare patch was hardly noticeable, the ornaments catching the light and creating a perfect balance of color and sparkle.

"See?" Olivia said proudly, pointing to various ornaments. "Doesn't it look even prettier today? And look—you can still see your church ornament right there, next to the heart!"

"It's still beautiful," Emma agreed, her voice thick with emotion. "You did such a wonderful job decorating it."

"We did." Mark corrected gently, coming to stand beside her. "It's perfect because we all worked on it together."

The moment was interrupted by Clair calling from the kitchen, "Dinner's ready! Eli, would you help me bring the dishes to the table?"

As they moved toward the dining room, Mark's hand found the small of Emma's back, guiding her gently. The touch was brief but electric, sending warmth spreading through her entire body.

The dining room table was set beautifully, with Mark's good china and flickering candles creating a warm, intimate atmosphere. Steam rose from the pot roast in the center of the table, surrounded by bowls of roasted vegetables, mashed potatoes, and homemade biscuits.

"Everything looks amazing," Emma said as they took their seats, Olivia insisting that Emma sit next to her.

"Thank you, dear," Clair replied, beaming. "Now, let's join hands and say grace."

They joined hands around the table, and Emma felt a flutter in her heart as Mark's warm fingers wrapped around hers on one side, while Olivia's small hand clasped her other. Eli's deep voice filled the room as he offered the blessing.

"Dear Heavenly Father, we thank you for this food and the hands that prepared it. We thank you for family, both old and new, and for bringing us together on this beautiful evening. We thank you for the gift of love, of second chances, and for your perfect timing in all things. Bless this food to our bodies and us to your service. In Jesus' name, Amen."

"Amen," they echoed, and Emma felt Mark squeeze her hand gently before letting go.

The meal was delicious. The pot roast was tender and flavorful, the vegetables perfectly seasoned, and the biscuits were indeed the best Emma had ever tasted. Conversation flowed easily, filled with laughter and stories, making Emma feel as though she'd always been part of these family dinners.

"Remember that Christmas when Mark tried to catch Santa?" Eli chuckled, passing the potatoes. "Must have been, what, third grade?"

Mark groaned good-naturedly. "I'd almost forgotten about that. I set up an elaborate trap with string and bells all around the Christmas tree."

"And ended up catching poor Patches instead," Clair added, referring to their old family cat. "That cat wouldn't come near the Christmas tree for years after that!"

Olivia giggled, clearly having heard this story before. "Daddy was silly when he was little, wasn't he, Miss Emma?"

"Well," Emma said, her eyes twinkling, "I seem to remember him doing some other silly things in high school, too."

"Oh?" Clair leaned forward, interested. "Do tell, dear."

Emma caught Mark's playful warning look and laughed. "Well, there was that time during the Christmas parade when he dressed up as an elf."

The stories and laughter continued through dinner and into dessert—a warm apple pie that made Emma think of childhood Christmases at her grandparent's house. As they finished their coffee, Olivia bounced in her seat, clearly ready for the next part of the evening.

"Can we read my new book now?" she asked hopefully. "Please?"

"Why don't we move to the living room?" Mark suggested. "It'll be cozier by the fire."

They moved to the living room, where the Christmas tree twinkled merrily in the corner and the fire cast a warm light over everything. Olivia immediately curled up next to Emma on the sofa, clutching her new book.

"Will you read it, Miss Emma? You do good voices—I can tell from when you help with the Christmas play," Olivia asked.

Emma looked at Mark, who nodded encouragingly as he settled into the armchair nearby. Eli and Clair sat nearby on the couch, Clair's knowing smile making Emma feel both nervous and completely at home.

Opening the book, Emma began to read, letting the familiar words flow naturally. "'Twas the night before Christmas, when all through the house..."

As she read, she found herself getting caught up in the magic of the story, doing different voices for each part, just as her father had done when she was young. Olivia snuggled closer, completely entranced, while the adults listened with warm appreciation.

Emma was aware of Mark watching her, his expression soft and full of something that made her heart beat faster. When she reached the final, "Merry Christmas to all, and to all, a good night!" Olivia sighed contentedly.

"That was perfect," she declared, hugging the book to her chest. "You read it just right, Miss Emma."

"She certainly did," Clair agreed, standing and stretching slightly. "But now, my dear, I believe it's getting late, and it's time for someone to get ready for bed."

"But I'm not tired," Olivia protested, even as she rubbed her eyes. "Can't Miss Emma read just one more story?"

Mark stood from his chair. "How about we save another story for another night? Remember, we have school tomorrow."

Emma's heart warmed at the implication that there would be other nights like this one. Olivia looked disappointed, but nodded, climbing off the couch.

"Will you come tuck me in?" she asked Emma hopefully.

Emma glanced at Mark, unsure if this crossed any boundaries, but his smile was warm and encouraging. "I think that would be nice," he said.

After saying goodnight to Eli and Clair, who were gathering their things to head home, Emma followed Mark and Olivia upstairs. Olivia's room was exactly as Emma had imagined it would be—warm and cozy, with twinkling fairy lights strung along the ceiling and walls covered in colorful artwork.

"Good night, Miss Emma," Olivia said, wrapping her arms around Emma's waist in a tight hug. "Thank you for my book and for reading it so good."

"Good night, sweetie," Emma replied. "Sweet dreams."

Mark tucked Olivia in, kissing her forehead and whispering something that made her giggle, before they both stepped out into the hallway. For a moment, they stood there in comfortable silence, the sounds of Eli and Clair leaving drifting up from downstairs.

"Thank you," Mark said quietly, "for everything tonight—the book, reading to her, just... being here. It means more than you know."

Emma's breath caught at the tenderness in his voice. "Thank you for including me. Your family is wonderful."

"They think you're wonderful too," Mark replied, his eyes meeting hers with an intensity that made her heart race. "I think... I think maybe we all know you were meant to be part of this somehow."

The weight of his words hung between them, full of possibility and promise.

"I should probably head home," she said reluctantly. "School tomorrow."

Mark nodded, leading the way downstairs. At the front door, he helped her with her coat, his fingers lingering slightly as he adjusted the collar.

"Drive safely," he said. "And Emma?"

She turned to face him, her hand on the doorknob. "Yes?"

"I'm really looking forward to Saturday—our proper date."

The way he said it, with such gentle certainty, made Emma's heart flip. "Me too," she admitted, and the smile that spread across his face was worth any uncertainty she might have felt.

As Emma drove home through the quiet streets of Laurel Ridge, she found herself smiling, remembering the warmth of the evening—the way Olivia had snuggled close as she read, the stories shared over dinner, the way Mark had looked at her when he thought she wasn't watching.

Maybe this was what coming home really meant—not just returning to a place, but finding where your heart had been waiting all along.

Chapter 21

Emma stepped into the familiar warmth of Martha's Diner, the chill of the December weather clinging to her as the door closed behind her.

She scanned the room for Leah, Wendy, and her mom, Penny, who had already settled into one of the far corner booths. The aroma of fresh coffee and baked apple pie drifted through the air, blending with the low murmur of conversations and the occasional clink of silverware.

Wendy spotted her first, raising a hand with a grin. "There she is! Managed to escape the school rush, I see."

Emma returned the smile, her pace quickening as she made her way over, tugging her scarf loose from her neck. "Barely," she sighed, sliding into the booth beside her mom as a new waitress deftly placed a steaming cup of coffee in front of her with a nod.

"Kids seem to get rowdier the closer we get to Christmas," Leah chuckled, her hands wrapped around her cup. "Like they can smell the vacation coming."

"Tell me about it. They're practically bouncing off the walls," Emma replied, gratefully taking a sip of her coffee.

Penny leaned back, a knowing smile tugging at the corners of her mouth. "You girls used to be the same way."

Emma shrugged, smiling as she glanced out the large window, watching people pass by on the sidewalks. "I can remember being so excited about Christmas break from school. And I remember the constant sleep-overs at each other's homes. All the baking and fun filled moments."

Wendy laughed, tucking a strand of hair behind her ear. "Oh, those were the days. Remember the year we tried to stay up all night baking Christmas cookies and ended up burning half of them because we fell asleep?"

Leah groaned, though the smile on her face said she remembered it fondly. "My mom was so mad. We stunk up the entire house!"

"Well, at least we learned how to use a fire extinguisher that night," Emma teased, earning a round of laughter from the table.

Penny shook her head, her eyes twinkling with nostalgia. "The things you girls got away with... I'm still amazed when I think of all the antics you pulled."

"Hey, we were creative!" Wendy protested, grinning. "Nothing wrong with a little adventure."

Emma wasn't really paying attention to the playful back-and-forth between her friends. Her mind drifted back to another Christmas, one not too long ago when she felt completely lost—like the world had stopped spinning when Rhett had died, and she was left to pick up the pieces. But now, there was a sense of peace blooming inside her, like seedling faith growing with care in the stillness of winter.

"Earth to Emma," Leah's voice broke into her thoughts. "We're losing you, girl. Come back to us."

Emma blinked, smiling sheepishly. "Sorry, I was just... thinking."

Wendy exchanged a look with Leah, a sly smile tugging at the corners of her mouth. "Thinking about someone in particular, maybe?"

Penny gave a knowing chuckle, patting Emma's hand. "Oh, honey, you've got that look."

"No, I do not have 'that look,'" Emma protested, though her cheeks betrayed her with how quickly they flushed.

"You've got it bad," Leah teased. "So? How's everything going with Mark and Olivia? Don't just leave us hanging!"

Emma toyed with the edge of the napkin that had come with her coffee, not quite knowing how to answer all at once. Her emotions were still packed tightly from what she and Mark had shared in the last week.

"It's just... good. Really good," Emma said, her fingers running absently along the handle of her mug. "It feels like everything I've been praying for. Like God's been leading me back to all the right places and all the right people."

Her mom gave her a warm smile, her eyes soft with understanding. "Sometimes, He brings you to things in ways you never expect, sweetheart."

"Exactly." Emma's voice caught slightly, glancing between her mom, Leah, and Wendy. "I never imagined I'd be back here, starting over with Mark, but... it feels right. Olivia is a blessing in disguise. And yet, all of it... it's happened so fast."

Penny's hand covered Emma's, that motherly strength always so comforting and steady. "You deserve all the joy that life—and love—can bring, Emma. Don't be afraid to embrace it."

"Olivia's so fond of you, too," Leah said.

"Fond? That little girl's practically attached to Emma at the hip," Wendy quipped before Emma could respond, smirking as she nudged her friend's shoulder. "I think you're a serious contender in the running for 'Most Awesome Stepmom.'"

Emma rolled her eyes but smiled, her heart swelling at the thought of Olivia. "She's... incredible," Emma admitted. "I've connected with her so quickly, and it's like there's already this unspoken bond between us. I love spending time with her."

"That's because you've got a big ol' momma heart, girl," Leah said with a wink. "Kids can always sense that. She knows you're safe."

Martha appeared, coffeepot in hand, and topped off each of their mugs with a knowing smile. "Sounds like some real heart talk happening over here." She winked at Emma, her voice laced with curiosity. "I heard a little rumor about you and Mark."

Emma groaned inwardly and glanced toward Wendy, who gave a sheepish shrug. It seemed nothing was sacred in a small town.

Martha leaned one hand on the edge of the table, her brow raised in a manner that suggested she wasn't letting things slide that easily. "So, am I going to hear the rest of this story from someone else, or from you?"

Emma sighed good-naturedly, unable to fight the warmth that spread through her chest. "We've been spending time together. It's... nice. More than nice, actually."

Penny gave Emma a little nudge, beaming at her daughter in encouragement. "She means they're falling in love all over again."

Emma shot her mom a playful glare before shaking her head. "Let's not rush things."

But Leah and Wendy exchanged yet another amused look.

"Too late!" Leah grinned. "It's obvious to everyone else, girl. Even if you don't see it yet... or want to admit it."

Martha chuckled, giving Emma a pat on the shoulder. "Well, I'll say we're all rooting for you around these parts. Got to love a good

Christmas romance, especially one that's got a real, lasting kind of love behind it."

Emma's stomach fluttered—part excitement, part nerves—but she spoke from the truth in her heart. "I think this time around, it's different. It feels deeper, like we're not just picking up where we left off, but really starting something new and meaningful. Something built on everything that's happened to us, all the heartache and the healing."

Martha nodded sagely, looking a little misty-eyed. "That's how you know it's the real thing."

"Yeah," Emma said, a smile spreading across her face. "I think you're right. It feels... good. It feels right. And you know what? I'm happy. Really, genuinely happy."

"Well, I'm thrilled to hear that," Martha said with a warm smile. "Now, what can I get you ladies to eat?"

The conversation shifted to lighter topics as Martha took orders. Emma smiled through it all, her heart savoring the truth of her earlier confession. Then came her mom's gentle pat on her hand again, reminding her of the safety and acceptance she'd found here in her small hometown, with the people who knew her best.

"So," Penny began, her eyes twinkling as she stirred her coffee, "What's the plan for you girls this evening?"

"Rehearsal for the Christmas play at the church," Emma replied with a smile, her fingers tracing the rim of her coffee cup.

"And while we're at the church, I've already brought over boxes of craft supplies and set them on a table, ready for anyone who'd like to help me sort through them in preparation for the Winter Festival.," Wendy chimed in. "I want to make sure we've got enough materials for the kids' craft area—we don't want to run short on anything festive."

"Speaking of the festival," Leah said with a smile, "you are coming, right, Emma?"

"Of course," Emma replied, her smile widening at the thought of the upcoming event. "Mark. Olivia and I are planning to go together."

Wendy's grin stretched from ear to ear. "Oh? Like an official date?" she teased.

Emma rolled her eyes, but it was impossible to suppress the blush that crept up her cheeks. "I suppose you could say that."

Martha arrived at their table again, her tray laden with plates of comfort food. She flashed a knowing smile as she set the warm dishes in front of them. "You girls better quit all this gab and hustle. Play practice starts in, what, thirty minutes?"

"Thirty-two, but who's counting?" Wendy quipped, quickly taking a bite of her chicken sandwich.

"Now, Penny, you make sure you keep these girls in line," Martha joked, with a playful gleam in her eye. She untied her apron with a practiced hand, signaling to the waitress who had served them coffee earlier. "I'm clocking out for the evening—I need to freshen up before heading to the church for play rehearsal. Sarah here," she nodded toward the waitress, "will take great care of y'all while I'm gone."

With a quick, conspiratorial wink, Martha hurried off, leaving the booth filled with lingering laughter and warm banter.

Chapter 22

The recreation hall buzzed with activity. Strings of twinkling white Christmas lights had been hung from the wooden beams above, casting a festive lighting over the stage where children, dressed as everything from angels to farm animals, ran through their rehearsals for the upcoming Christmas play.

Laughter, high-pitched and uncontainable, echoed through the space. Emma smiled as she adjusted the crooked halo on Miranda Newman's head, the tallest third-grader, who was currently fussing with her white, feathered angel wings.

"There you go," Emma said warmly, kneeling to adjust the ribbon that tied the halo in place. "Now you look like the perfect Christmas angel."

Miranda beamed, her freckled cheeks pinking with excitement. "Do you think I'll remember to say my line this time, Miss Emma? I keep forgetting the part after, 'Glory to God in the highest.'"

"You'll do great. Just take a deep breath and listen for the music. And remember, even angels need to breathe." Emma offered an encouraging smile, giving the girl's shoulder a reassuring squeeze, before Miranda bounded off to join the other angels lining up at the side of the stage.

She stepped back, surveying the scene. Little shepherds practiced their march toward the faux manger, giggles loud enough that even the plywood stable seemed to sway in amusement. Several wise men fiddled with their paper crowns, while Mary and Joseph—Justin and Amber, both fourth graders—practiced cradling a baby doll meticulously wrapped in one of Martha's hand-knitted baby blankets. The whole thing was adorable, messy, and utterly heartwarming.

It was chaos wrapped in Christmas joy.

Emma suppressed a laugh as one of the smaller angels, Isabelle Foster, ran toward her at full speed with a pair of oversized angel wings that seemed to swallow her entire body. "Miss Emma, my wings are too big! They keep bumping into all the other angels!"

Looking down into the girl's wide, pleading eyes, Emma bit her lip to keep from laughing outright. "Alright, let's see if we can fix that, shall we?" She crouched down, working quickly to secure the wings tighter around Isabelle's tiny shoulders, offering soothing words as she worked.

"Better?" she asked, finally standing and admiring her handiwork.

Isabelle spun in a small circle, nodding enthusiastically. "Much better! Thank you, Miss Emma!"

"You're welcome, sweetheart," Emma said, grinning at Isabelle's exuberance. "Now go show off those wings."

The little girl ran off, her giggles blending into the joyful hum of the hall once more.

"Might be the first time I've seen one of these pint-sized angels stay in one spot for longer than five seconds." Mark's deep voice cut through the flurry of noise, his presence sending an immediate spark through Emma.

She glanced up in time to see him approaching, Olivia skipping just behind him. Olivia's cheeks were flushed red from excitement, her wings slightly lopsided and held together by an abundance of safety pins.

"Hi, Miss Emma!" Olivia greeted, adjusting one of her feathered wings where it sagged under the weight of pins. "Look, my wings are almost as big as Isabelle's, but not too big. Right, Daddy?"

Mark chuckled, bending down to a few of her pins. "All those safety pins would make your grandma proud." He glanced sidelong at Emma, his eyes twinkling. "Or maybe she'll give me an earful about using up all her sewing notions when she sees this."

Emma laughed, watching Mark's deft hands as they worked with the pins. There was something undeniably charming about this man—a widowed father who somehow managed to juggle his daughter's boundless energy and his own quiet strength with such grace.

"Come on, Daddy! I want Miss Emma to see me practice my angel entrance." Olivia hopped up after the pins were fixed, pulling on her father's sleeve. "Come on, pleeeaase?"

"I'm coming." Mark smiled, standing to follow his daughter with a playful sigh.

As they approached the stage, Olivia turned and beckoned for Emma to follow. "Miss Emma, come with us! You said angels need an audience, too."

With a soft laugh, Emma nodded and followed Olivia closer to the front of the stage area. Mark beside her, their hands brushing lightly as they walked.

"You've got a loyal fan in her now, you know," Mark whispered, leaning toward Emma. His voice was warm, laced with affection, and the sound of it made her pulse quicken. "She talks about you constantly at home. You're her favorite angel wrangler, hands down."

Emma chuckled, blushing as she looked toward Olivia, who had taken her place at the side of the stage, her face scrunched in intense concentration as she awaited her cue. "I think she's more of a natural at this than some of us, to be honest. You should've seen me at her age—couldn't keep my halo or wings on to save my life."

Mark's soft laughter filled the space between them, and for a moment, Emma wished time could pause right there, with Olivia smiling on stage and their shared warmth buzzing in the air like quiet electricity.

Just then, Martha Kincaid—larger than life and full of holiday cheer—made her entrance into the hall, clapping her hands loudly as she half-shouted above the hubbub of excited children. "Alright, kiddos! Places everyone—a Christmas play waits for no one!"

The kids scrambled to attention, some more disciplined than others. Martha somehow managed to organize the delightful chaos.

Martha, ever full of witty sass, turned toward Emma with a sly grin. "Well now, don't you two look cute"—her gaze flickered between Emma and Mark.

Emma's blush deepened, and Mark laughed heartily at the comment before quickly stepping in to shift the focus back to the rehearsal. "Okay, kids!" Mark called out, his playful tone laced with seriousness. "Let's take it from the top! Angels, remember your cues—shepherds, you're on deck after the wise men."

As the children settled into their positions, Olivia came bounding over to Emma, grabbing her hand and pulling her toward one of the folding chairs at the very edge of the stage. "You'll watch, right? You said you'd watch!"

"I wouldn't miss it for the world," Emma reassured her, squeezing Olivia's small hand affectionately before taking a seat.

Olivia's voice lifted as the play's soft music cue began beneath the melody of jingling bells. Her little halo tilted slightly as she stepped into the floodlight, reciting her lines perfectly and proudly. The purity in her performance—the innocence in the way she beamed at Emma as she stood bathed in light—tugged at Emma's heart.

After Olivia's angelic performance, she rushed back to Emma as soon as her scene ended, flinging her arms around Emma's waist. "Did you see me? Did you see it?"

"I saw every second, and you were amazing," Emma told her sincerely, running her fingers through the little girl's honey-brown hair.

"You're like... really special, Miss Emma." Olivia said thoughtfully, looking up at Emma with wide, adoring eyes.

Emma's heart swelled, and she gazed down at Olivia with a tender smile. "Thank you, sweetheart." Emma replied as Olivia was called back upstage for the shepherd scene.

"She's adorable," Emma said as she leaned toward Mark, folding her arms in front of her, keeping her voice low to not disturb the rehearsal.

"She gets that from her mom," Mark said, and when his gaze dropped to meet Emma's, there was no sadness there—just appreciation for the present moment.

His fingers brushed hers as he handed her a piece of paper with a quick edit to the script the kids had been working on.

"Miss Emma! Daddy! Can you please help me with the shepherd's staff? It's stuck in my sleeve!"

"Crisis averted," Mark said playfully as they walked together to where Olivia awaited their help, her face scrunched in frustration as she tried untangling the staff from her costume.

"Let me help you, sweetie," Emma said, dropping to her knees and carefully working through the tangled mess. "Next time, maybe a shepherd without the long sleeves."

Olivia giggled, still bright.

For the rest of the rehearsal, they worked together, hand-in-hand with the other parents, helping the children through their paces, and adjusting costumes until everything was just as it should be.

As the evening wound down, and the last of the children gathered their things for home, Mark sidled up to Emma once more.

"You've really got the makings of a shepherd for lost sheep, you know," he murmured with a smile, his eyes warm under the twinkling Christmas lights. "I'd say some of us need that more than we realize."

Chapter 23

The rest of the week passed in a flurry of holiday activities and anticipation. Between helping with Christmas play rehearsals at the church, tending to the usual parade of students in her office, and trying to contain her growing excitement about Saturday's festival, Emma barely noticed how quickly the days flew by.

On Friday, as Emma carefully placed a bandage on a kindergartener's scraped knee, Wendy appeared in the doorway, bouncing with excitement.

"There," Emma said to the little girl, smoothing the bandage. "All better. Remember to be careful and no more running in the halls, okay?"

After the child skipped away, Wendy closed the door and turned to Emma with a grin. "So, tomorrow's the big day! Have you decided what you're wearing to the festival?"

Emma groaned, sinking into her chair. "Is it silly that I've been thinking about that all week? I want to look nice, but it needs to be practical for ice skating and being outdoors..."

"Which is exactly why I'm here," Wendy declared, perching on the edge of Emma's desk. "Emergency shopping trip after school. No arguments."

"Wendy, I have plenty of clothes—"

"Emma Louise Whitman," Wendy cut in, using her best stern voice, "this is your first proper date with Mark Thompson in years. You're going to let me help you find something perfect, and you're going to enjoy it."

Emma laughed, knowing resistance was futile. "Fine, but nothing too fancy. It's just the Winter Festival."

"It's not 'just' anything," Wendy corrected. "Now, what time is he picking you up tomorrow?"

"Three o'clock," Emma replied, trying to ignore the flutter in her stomach. "He said that way we'll have time to enjoy the festival before the tree lighting ceremony at dusk."

Wendy's eyes sparkled. "Perfect. The tree lighting is always so romantic. Remember when we were pre-teens, and we used to dream about finding the perfect guy to kiss under those twinkling lights?"

"Wendy!" Emma felt her cheeks warm.

"What? I'm just saying, some dreams have a way of coming true—even if they take a little longer than we expected."

After school, Emma was whisked away to Laurel Ridge's charming shopping district. The streets were decorated for Christmas, with garlands strung between lampposts and twinkling lights in every shop window. Snow had been carefully shoveled from the sidewalks, and the late afternoon sun provided a little warmth and cheer.

"Here we are," Wendy announced, pulling Emma into Mountain Chic Boutique, a local clothing store that had been a fixture in Laurel Ridge for years. A small bell chimed as they entered, and warm air scented with cinnamon and vanilla enveloped them.

"Wendy! Emma!" Beth Rutledge, the shop owner, called out from behind the counter. "I knew you were stopping by today. I just got in some beautiful sweaters that would be perfect for tomorrow's festival."

Emma smiled, touched but not surprised that Beth knew about her upcoming date. News traveled fast in Laurel Ridge.

"That's exactly why we're here," Wendy said, already heading toward a display of winter wear. "Emma needs something special."

The next hour was a whirlwind of trying on clothes, with Wendy and Beth offering enthusiastic opinions on each outfit. Finally, they settled on a soft, rose-colored sweater dress that hit just above Emma's knees, paired with warm leggings and a cream-colored scarf.

"It's perfect," Wendy declared as Emma appeared from the fitting room. "Festive, but practical, and that color makes your eyes look amazing."

Emma had to admit, looking in the mirror, that the outfit was exactly right. The sweater dress was comfortable enough for ice skating but still feminine and pretty. The color brought a natural flush to her cheeks, making her look... happy and alive.

"You look beautiful, dear," Beth said, adjusting the scarf slightly. "Mark won't know what hit him."

Emma blushed but couldn't hide her smile. After paying for the outfit, they stepped back onto the street, where the early winter evening was settling in.

"Coffee?" Wendy suggested, nodding toward the small cafe across the street. "We should celebrate your successful shopping trip."

They found a cozy corner table in the cafe, and soon were warming their hands around steaming mugs of peppermint-flavored coffee. Through the window, they could see workers setting up booths in the town square for tomorrow's festival.

"Are you nervous?" Wendy asked, studying Emma's face.

Emma considered the question, watching as a group of volunteers strung lights around the massive Christmas tree that would be lit tomorrow night. "A little," she admitted. "But not in a bad way. More like... butterfly nervous. Excited nervous."

"That's good," Wendy smiled. "You deserve this, Emma. You deserve to be excited and happy about something again."

"It's just..." Emma paused, gathering her thoughts. "Everything feels so right, you know? Being back here, spending time with Mark and Olivia, even helping with the Christmas play. It's like all these pieces are falling into place, and part of me is just waiting for something to go wrong."

"Oh, honey," Wendy reached across the table and squeezed Emma's hand. "That's just fear talking."

Emma nodded, remembering Eli's grace at dinner the other night, thanking God for second chances. "You're right. I know you're right. I just need to trust."

"And maybe," Wendy added with a twinkle in her eye, "trust that sometimes the best Christmas presents are the ones we never saw coming."

They finished their coffee as darkness settled over Laurel Ridge, the Christmas lights now casting a magical glow over the town square. As they walked to their cars, Wendy pulled Emma into a tight hug.

"You're going to have a wonderful time tomorrow," she said firmly. "Just remember to breathe, be yourself, and trust that everything is happening exactly as it should."

That night, as Emma hung her new outfit in her closet, her phone buzzed with a text from Mark:

"Just checking—still on for tomorrow? Olivia's already laid out her festival outfit and is too excited to sleep."

Emma smiled, typing back: *"Definitely still on. Tell Olivia sweet dreams, and I can't wait to see her festival outfit."*

His response came quickly: *"She's not the only one looking forward to tomorrow. Sleep well, Emma."*

As Emma got ready for bed, she hummed Christmas carols, her heart full of anticipation for tomorrow. Through her window, she could see the lights of the town square twinkling in the distance, and somewhere in that glow was the promise of something beautiful.

She fell asleep thinking of twinkling lights, the sound of carols, and the way Mark's eyes crinkled when he smiled—all the magical pieces of a dream she'd never dared to wish for coming true.

Chapter 24

Saturday afternoon arrived with perfect winter weather—crisp and cold but not bitter, with occasional snowflakes drifting lazily from a blue sky. Emma stood in front of her mirror, adjusting her new sweater dress and taking one last look at her reflection. The butterfly nervous feeling in her stomach had intensified, but in a way that made her feel alive and expectant rather than anxious.

A knock at her bedroom door preceded Andrew poking his head in. "Mark just pulled up," he said, then grinned at her expression. "You look beautiful, sis."

"Thanks," Emma replied, giving her scarf one final tweak. "How's the weather holding up?"

"Perfect for the festival. Cold enough to keep the ice rink frozen, but not so cold that people won't want to be outside." He paused, his expression softening. "You know, I haven't seen you this happy in so long."

Emma felt tears prick at her eyes and blinked them away quickly. "I am happy," she admitted. "Really happy."

Another knock echoed through the house—this time from the front door. Emma's heart did a little flip as she grabbed her coat and purse.

"Have fun," Andrew called after her as she headed downstairs. "Remember, I'm blessing this union!"

"Andrew!" Emma laughed, shaking her head at her brother's teasing.

She opened the front door to find Mark and Olivia waiting on the porch. Mark looked handsome in a dark blue sweater and jeans, a warm coat hanging open despite the cold. But it was Olivia who immediately captured Emma's attention—she was practically bouncing with excitement, wearing a red wool dress with white tights and a matching red bow in her hair.

"Miss Emma!" Olivia exclaimed. "You look so pretty! Doesn't she look pretty, Daddy?"

Mark's eyes met Emma's, warm and appreciative. "Beautiful," he said softly, and Emma felt her cheeks flush.

"You look very pretty too, Olivia," Emma said, loving how the little girl beamed at the compliment. "That bow is perfect for the festival."

"Ready to go?" Mark asked, offering his arm in a playfully gallant gesture that made Emma laugh.

"Ready," she confirmed, slipping her arm through his while Olivia skipped ahead of them to the truck.

The drive to town was filled with Olivia's excited chatter about all the festival activities she wanted to do—decorating cookies at Wendy's booth, visiting the petting zoo, ice skating, and, of course, seeing the tree lighting ceremony.

As they approached the town square, Emma could see that Laurel Ridge had outdone itself this year. The entire square was transformed into a winter wonderland, with more strings of white lights creating a canopy overhead. Wooden booths lined the periphery, offering everything from hot chocolate to handmade crafts. The ice rink had been set up in the center, and the massive Christmas tree stood proudly near the gazebo, waiting for its moment to shine.

They found a parking spot, and as they walked toward the festival, Olivia walking slightly ahead of them. Emma felt Mark's hand brush against hers. Without hesitation, she linked her fingers with his, feeling a wave of warmth spread through her despite the cold air.

"Ice skating first?" Olivia suggested hopefully. "Before it gets too crowded?"

Mark looked at Emma, squeezing her hand gently. "What do you think? Ready to test your skating skills?"

"As ready as I'll ever be," Emma laughed. "Just remember your promise not to let me fall."

They made their way to the rental booth, where they were given ice skates in their sizes. Emma sat next to Olivia on a bench, helping her lace up her skates.

"Don't worry, Miss Emma," Olivia said seriously as they stood carefully. "Daddy's really good at skating. He won't let either of us fall."

True to his word, Mark proved to be a steady support as they made their way onto the ice. He kept one hand firmly clasped with Emma's while Olivia glided ahead of them, already comfortable on her skates.

"I used to do this all the time as a kid," Emma said, slowly finding her balance. "How is it I've forgotten everything?"

Mark chuckled, his breath visible in the cold air. "It's like riding a bike—it'll come back to you. Just keep holding on to me."

The way he said it, soft and sure, made Emma's heart flutter. She tightened her grip on his hand as they began to move around the rink, following Olivia's path.

Gradually, Emma began to remember the rhythm of skating. The ice gleamed beneath their feet, and the late afternoon sun caught the occasional snowflake, making it sparkle like diamond dust. Christmas music played softly from speakers around the square, and the smell of hot chocolate filled the air.

"See?" Mark said after they'd made a few circuits. "You're getting it."

Emma smiled, feeling more confident.

"Miss Emma!" Olivia called, skating back to them. "Watch this!" She demonstrated a small twirl, wobbling slightly but staying upright.

"Careful, peanut," Mark cautioned, though he was smiling proudly.

They spent the next hour on the ice, with Olivia showing off her developing skating skills, while Mark and Emma moved together in comfortable synchronization. By the time they took a break, Emma's cheeks were flushed from both the cold and laughter.

"Hot chocolate?" Mark suggested as they returned their skates. "I think we've earned it."

They made their way to Martha's booth, where she was serving her famous hot chocolate with homemade marshmallows in the shape of stars. The warm cups felt heavenly in their chilly hands as they walked through the festival, stopping to admire various displays and greeting friends along the way.

"Look!" Olivia pointed excitedly. "There's the cookie decorating station! Can we do that next?"

The booth, run by Wendy and several other ladies from church, was set up with dozens of sugar cookies ready to be decorated. Olivia immediately dove in, covering her cookie with enough edible glitter to make it sparkle like a disco ball.

"Some things never change," Mark murmured in Emma's ear as they watched. "She gets her decorating style from me, I'm afraid."

Emma laughed. "I think it's perfect," she said. "Sometimes the most beautiful things are the ones that shine the brightest."

Mark turned to her, his voice soft yet filled with sincerity. "I couldn't agree more, Emma."

Before she could respond, they were interrupted by a familiar voice.

"Well, if it isn't my favorite festival-goers!" Clair approached, wearing a festive red coat. "Are you enjoying yourselves?"

"Grandma!" Olivia abandoned her cookie decorating to give Clair a hug, leaving a trail of glitter in her wake. "Look what I made!"

As Olivia showed off her creation, Emma felt Mark's arm slip around her waist, natural and protective against the growing evening chill. She leaned into him slightly, savoring the warmth and rightness of the moment.

"The tree lighting will start soon," Clair said, checking her watch. "You'll want to find a good spot. It's going to be beautiful this year—we've added some special touches."

They made their way toward the town Christmas tree, finding a perfect viewing spot near the gazebo. The sun had nearly set, casting a purple-blue twilight over the square. The crowd grew as more families gathered, and the excitement was palpable in the air.

Olivia stood in front of Mark and Emma, who kept their arms around her to keep her warm. As they waited, the town choir began singing carols, their voices rising clear and beautiful in the winter air.

"This is my favorite part," Olivia whispered, leaning back against them. "When everything gets quiet and then the tree lights up like magic."

Emma felt Mark's arm tighten around her waist as Eli stepped forward to lead the lighting ceremony. His voice carried across the square, strong and full of warmth, as he spoke about the meaning of Christmas, about light coming into darkness, and about the power of love to transform everything it touches.

"And now," Eli's voice rang out across the hushed crowd, "let us remember that just as this tree brings light to our town square, the true light of Christmas—God's love—brings hope and joy to our hearts. Let the lighting of this tree remind us that even in the darkest times, love and light will always find a way to shine through."

A countdown began, led by the children in the crowd. Olivia's voice joined in enthusiastically.

"Ten... nine... eight..."

Emma felt Mark's hand find hers in the growing darkness.

"Seven... six... five..."

Snowflakes began to fall more steadily now, catching the last remnants of twilight.

"Four... three... two..."

Mark's thumb brushed across her knuckles gently, sending warmth spreading through her despite the cold.

"One!"

The tree blazed to life, thousands of white lights twinkling from base to star, casting a magical light over the gathered crowd. A collective gasp of wonder rose from the square, followed by applause and cheers. The choir began singing "O Holy Night," their voices rising pure and clear into the snowy evening.

"It's beautiful," Emma whispered, watching as the lights seemed to dance through the falling snow.

"Yes, it is," Mark replied softly, but when she turned to look at him, she found him watching her instead of the tree. The twinkling lights reflected in his eyes, and something in his expression made her heart skip.

"Look!" Olivia's excited voice broke the moment as she pointed upward. "The star! It's so bright."

They all looked up at the giant star adorning the top of the tree, its golden light seeming to reach out into the darkness like a beacon of hope.

As the choir continued singing, families began to disperse to various activities around the square. Some headed for the refreshment stands, others toward the carousel that had been set up near the edge of the square, its lights spinning in colorful circles through the snow.

"Can we ride the carousel?" Olivia asked hopefully. "Just once before we go home?"

"Of course, Liv," Mark smiled. "Why don't you go with Gigi? She's right over there. I'm sure she'd love to ride with you."

Olivia looked between them with surprising perception for a seven-year-old. "Okay," she agreed easily. "You and Miss Emma can watch from here. The tree is prettier from this spot, anyway."

As Olivia skipped off toward Clair, who welcomed her with open arms, Mark turned to Emma. The music had shifted to "Silent Night," and the snow was falling steadily now, creating a soft, magical curtain around them.

"Dance with me?" he asked quietly, holding out his hand.

Emma's heart fluttered as she placed her hand in his. "Here? Now?"

"Why not?" His smile was gentle as he drew her close, one hand settling at her waist while the other held hers against his chest. "It's perfect."

And it was. They swayed together slowly, the carol washing over them as snowflakes danced in the glow of the Christmas tree. Emma could see Olivia on the carousel, waving each time she passed. Her face lit up with joy. Couples and families moved around the square, everything softened by the falling snow and twinkling lights.

"Emma," Mark's voice was soft but serious, making her look up at him. "I need to tell you something."

Her heart quickened at his tone. "What is it?"

He took a deep breath, his eyes never leaving hers. "I think I'm falling in love with you. Again. Or maybe I never really stopped in the first place." He paused, his hand tightening slightly on her waist. I know it might be too soon to say it, and I don't expect you to say anything back. I just... I needed you to know. Being with you these past few weeks, seeing you with Olivia, watching you become part of our lives again—it's shown me what I've been missing all these years."

Emma felt tears prick at her eyes, but they weren't sad tears. They were the kind that came when your heart was so full it couldn't hold all the emotion anymore.

"Mark," she whispered, her voice trembling slightly. "I—"

But before she could finish, Olivia came running back, her cheeks pink with cold and excitement. "Daddy! Miss Emma! Did you see me on the carousel? I rode the pretty white horse."

Mark laughed, keeping one arm around Emma as he scooped Olivia up with the other. "We saw you, sweetheart. You looked like a princess up there."

Emma watched them together, her heart so full it felt like it might burst. This was what coming home felt like—not just to a place, but to people who made your soul feel complete.

As they walked back to the truck, Olivia between them, holding both their hands and chattering about the evening's adventures, Emma caught Mark's eye. The love she saw there wasn't just for Olivia anymore—it was for her too, patient and steady and sure.

And in that moment, surrounded by falling snow and Christmas lights, Emma realized something important: sometimes the best gifts weren't the ones wrapped in paper and bows, but the ones that came wrapped in second chances and God's perfect timing.

Chapter 25

The drive home was quiet and peaceful, with Olivia dozing in the back seat, worn out from all the excitement. Christmas music played softly on the radio, and the headlights cut through the gently falling snow, creating a tunnel of whirling white flakes before them.

Emma stole glances at Mark as he drove, remembering his words from earlier. Her heart felt full to bursting with everything she wanted to say back to him, but hadn't had the chance to express.

They pulled up to the parsonage all too soon. Mark turned to check on Olivia, who was sound asleep.

"I should probably get her home to bed," he said, but made no move to leave. Instead, he turned to face Emma fully. "Thank you for coming with us tonight. It wouldn't have been the same without you."

Emma smiled, warmth spreading through her chest. "Thank you for asking me. It was perfect—all of it."

They sat in comfortable silence for a moment; the snow creating a private little world around them. Finally, Mark spoke again, his voice gentle but certain.

"About what I said earlier... I meant it, Emma. Every word. I know it might seem fast, or complicated because of our history, but—"

"I love you too," Emma interrupted softly, the words falling from her lips as naturally as breathing. "I think maybe I always have, even when I tried not to. Being here, with you and Olivia... it feels right. Like this is exactly where I'm supposed to be."

Mark's breath caught audibly, and his hand found hers in the darkness of the truck cab. "Yeah?"

"Yeah, she confirmed, squeezing his fingers. "I was so scared to feel this way again, after everything that happened with Rhett. But being with you... it's different. It feels like coming home."

Mark lifted their joined hands to his lips, pressing a gentle kiss to her knuckles. "We'll take it slow," he promised. "One day at a time. But Emma... I want you to know that whatever happens, whatever this becomes, you're already part of our family. You and Olivia, you're my entire world now."

A small sound from the back seat made them both turn. Olivia had shifted in her sleep, a peaceful smile on her face as she clutched the stuffed reindeer she'd brought from home.

"I should get her home," Mark said reluctantly, though he made no move to let go of Emma's hand.

"Text me when you get there?" Emma asked, and Mark's smile widened.

"Of course." He hesitated for a moment, then leaned across the console slowly, giving her plenty of time to pull away if she wanted to. Instead, Emma met him halfway.

The kiss was soft and sweet, full of promise and possibility. It tasted like hot chocolate and winter air and coming home all at once. When they pulled apart, Mark rested his forehead against hers for a moment.

"Good night, Emma," he whispered.

"Good night," she replied, her heart singing with joy.

She watched from her front door as they drove away; the snow swirling in their wake. Inside, she found Andrew waiting up, pretending to read but clearly eager to hear about her evening.

"So?" he asked, trying and failing to look casual. "Good night?"

Emma touched her lips, still feeling the warmth of Mark's kiss. "Perfect night," she said softly. "Flawless."

Later, as she got ready for bed, her phone buzzed with a text from Mark:

"Home safe. Olivia woke up just enough to tell me this was 'the best festival ever' before falling back asleep. I have to agree with her. Sweet dreams, Emma. I love you."

Emma hugged the phone to her chest, feeling as though her heart might burst with happiness. Through her window, she could see the snow still falling, each flake catching the moonlight like a tiny star. Everything felt magical and new, yet somehow as familiar as an old Christmas carol.

This, she realized, was what she'd been searching for all along—not just love, but the kind of love that felt like faith and family and future all wrapped up together. The kind of love that felt like God's perfect plan unfolding exactly as it should.

Chapter 26

Monday morning dawned bright and clear, the weekend's snow sparkling like diamond dust in the early sunlight. Emma hummed to herself as she organized supplies in her office, still floating on the happiness of Saturday night. Her phone buzzed with a text from Mark:

"Good morning. Coffee in my classroom before first bell?"

Emma's heart did a little flip as she replied: *"Be there in five."*

The halls were still quiet as she made her way to Mark's classroom. Most students had not yet arrived for the day. She found him at his desk, two steaming travel mugs waiting beside him.

"Hi," he said, standing as she entered, his smile warming her all the way to her toes.

"Hi," she replied, accepting the coffee he offered. Their fingers brushed during the exchange, and even that small touch sent sparks through her.

"Sleep well?" he asked, leaning against his desk as she perched on the edge of a student's desk nearby.

"Very well," she smiled. "Though someone kept texting me sweet messages that made it hard to fall asleep."

Mark's eyes crinkled at the corners. "Guilty as charged. But I couldn't help it—everything still feels a bit like a dream."

"A good dream," Emma added softly.

"The best," he agreed, moving to stand closer to her. "Speaking of dreams... Olivia has a request."

"Oh?"

"She wants to know if you'll help us bake Christmas cookies this weekend. Apparently, our usual sugar cookies aren't fancy enough anymore, not after seeing the ones at the festival."

Emma laughed, remembering Olivia's enthusiasm at the decorating booth. "I'd love to. Let's do it at the parsonage for a change. Though I should warn you, I'm really getting into a glitter and sprinkles stage in my cookie decorating life."

"I think we can handle it," Mark said, his voice dropping slightly as he moved even closer. "As long as you don't mind possibly getting a little flour in your hair."

Emma's breath caught at his proximity. "I'm sure I'll manage—"

A sudden burst of chatter from the hallway interrupted them as the first students began arriving for the day. Mark stepped back slightly, though his eyes still held hers with warming intensity.

"This weekend, then?" he confirmed. "Saturday afternoon?"

"It's a date," Emma agreed, gathering her coffee and heading toward the door. She paused in the doorway, looking back at him. "Oh, and Mark?"

"Hmm?"

"I love you too," she said, echoing his last text from the night before.

The smile that spread across his face was brighter than the morning sun.

The week settled into a comfortable rhythm, though everything felt different now, colored by the warmth of renewed love and possibility. Emma and Mark shared lunch in his classroom each day with Olivia, who seemed to glow with happiness at having them both together. They exchanged texts throughout the day—little moments of connection that made Emma's heart lighter with each buzz of her phone.

Wednesday evening found them in the recreation hall behind the church, overseeing the Christmas play rehearsal. Emma sat in the front row beside Mark, making notes about costumes while he reviewed the script with the students on stage.

"Okay, angels," Mark called out, "remember to wait for your cue before coming in. Mary and Joseph need to reach the manger first."

Emma watched as Olivia, in her angel costume, practiced her entrance with the other children. Her heart swelled at the sight of Mark directing the rehearsal, his patience, and gentle encouragement bringing out the best in each child.

"You're good at this," she said softly when he sat down beside her during a break. "Working with the kids, making them feel confident."

"They make it easy," he replied modestly. "They just need someone to believe in them." He paused, then added with a smile, "Kind of like how someone once believed in me, even when I didn't believe in myself."

Emma felt tears prick at her eyes, remembering their conversation about why he'd left years ago. Before she could respond, Olivia came bounding down from the stage.

"Daddy! Miss Emma! Was that better? I remembered to wait for my cue this time!"

"It was perfect, sweetheart," Mark assured her, pulling her into a quick hug. "You're going to be the best angel in the show."

"That's because Miss Emma helped me practice," Olivia declared proudly. "She knows all about angels because she's kind of like one herself."

Emma's heart melted at the simple, innocent compliment. She caught Mark's eye and found him watching her with such tenderness it made her breath catch.

"You might be right about that, Liv," he said softly, his gaze never leaving Emma's face.

Thursday brought a fresh dusting of snow and a surprise visit from Clair during Emma's lunch break. She appeared in the doorway of Emma's office carrying a covered dish that smelled heavenly.

"I thought you might like some of my chicken soup," Clair said warmly. "The weather's turning colder, and there's nothing better than homemade soup on a winter day."

"Thank you," Emma replied, touched by the thoughtful gesture. "You didn't have to do that."

"Nonsense," Clair waved off her protests, settling into the chair across from Emma's desk. "Looking after family is what I do best."

The word 'family' sent a warm flutter through Emma's heart. Clair's eyes twinkled as she watched Emma's reaction.

"You know," she continued, her voice gentle, "I've been praying for this for a long time—for both you and Mark to find your way back to each other. Sometimes God's timing isn't what we expect, but it's always perfect."

Emma felt tears prick at her eyes. "I'm beginning to understand that," she said softly. "Being here, with Mark and Olivia... it feels like coming home in a way I never expected."

"Love has a way of doing that," Clair agreed. "And speaking of love, I heard you're coming over this weekend for Christmas cookie baking?"

Emma laughed. "Yes, though I'm a bit nervous about living up to Olivia's expectations."

"Oh, don't worry about that," Clair assured her. "That child thinks everything you do is magical. You should hear her talk about you at Sunday school—'Miss Emma this' and 'Miss Emma that.' You've captured her heart completely." She paused, her expression softening. "Just like you've captured her father's."

Before Emma could respond, there was a knock at her door. Mark stood there, holding his own lunch bag and wearing a warm smile.

"Hope I'm not interrupting," he said, stepping into the office. "I thought we might have lunch together again, since Olivia decided she wanted to eat with her friends in the cafeteria today."

"Perfect timing," Clair stood, gathering her purse. "I was just dropping off some soup for Emma. You two enjoy your lunch." She winked at Emma before heading out, leaving them alone.

Mark moved closer, setting his lunch on Emma's desk. "Everything okay? You look a little emotional."

"Happy emotional," Emma assured him, reaching for his hand. "Your mom was just... being your mom. Making me feel like family."

Mark's expression softened as he squeezed her fingers. "You are family," he said simply. "In all the ways that matter."

They shared lunch together, talking about the upcoming Christmas play, weekend plans, and all the small, precious details of their daily lives. Emma marveled at how natural it felt, sharing these quiet moments with him.

"Oh, I almost forgot," Mark said as they were cleaning up. "Olivia has a special request for our cookie baking session."

"Another one?" Emma laughed. "What is it this time?"

"She wants to make cookies for Santa, but not just any cookies. She wants to make ones that tell our story—whatever that means in the mind of a seven-year-old."

Emma's heart melted at the thought. "That's actually really sweet. We could do angels for her part in the play, maybe a Christmas tree for the night we all decorated together..."

"And a heart," Mark added softly, "for the moment I realized I was falling in love with you all over again."

Emma felt her cheeks warm as she met his gaze. "When was that moment?" she asked quietly.

"Honestly? Remember when we bumped into each other in the hallway? It was like everything just... clicked into place. Like my heart remembered something my head had tried to forget," he said.

Emma stood from her desk, moving around to where he sat. Without hesitation, she leaned down and kissed him softly, pouring all her emotions into the gentle pressure of her lips against his.

When they pulled apart, Mark's eyes were bright with emotion. "What was that for?"

"For being you," Emma replied simply. "For giving us a second chance. For loving me enough to say it first."

The warning bell rang, signaling the end of lunch, but neither of them moved for a moment, lost in each other's eyes.

"I should go," Mark said reluctantly. "Fourth graders wait for no man."

Emma laughed, stepping back to let him stand. "Go teach. I'll see you after school?"

"Count on it," he promised, stealing one more quick kiss before heading to the door. He paused in the doorway, looking back at her with a gaze that made her heart skip. "By the way, Mom's right. You are magical—to all of us."

With that, he disappeared into the hallway, leaving Emma standing in her office with a smile she couldn't suppress if she tried. Through her window, she could see the winter sun glinting off the fresh snow, creating tiny rainbows that seemed to dance in celebration of this perfect moment.

She touched her lips, still feeling the warmth of his kiss, and whispered a quiet prayer of gratitude. For second chances, for divine timing, and for the kind of love that felt like coming home.

The rest of the week stretched before her, filled with promise—cookie baking with Olivia, Christmas play rehearsals, and countless small moments with Mark that would weave together to create something even more beautiful and lasting.

Chapter 27

Saturday morning arrived with a crisp, clear winter sky that seemed to sparkle with possibility. Emma stood in the parsonage kitchen, gathering supplies for their cookie-baking adventure, while Christmas music played softly in the background.

Her phone buzzed with a text from Mark: *"Olivia's been up since dawn, asking every five minutes if it's time to go to your house yet. Should we head over early?"*

Emma smiled, typing back: *"Please do. Everything's ready here."*

While waiting for them to arrive, she finished setting out ingredients on the counter—flour, sugar, vanilla, and all the decorating supplies she could find. She'd even picked up a few special cookie cutters the day before, knowing how excited Olivia would be to make cookies that matched her role in the play.

The doorbell rang, and Emma could hear Olivia's excited chatter even before she opened the door. There they stood, Mark and Olivia, both rosy-cheeked from the cold, with matching smiles that warmed Emma from the inside out.

"Miss Emma!" Olivia burst through the door, practically bouncing with excitement. "I brought my apron! And Daddy says I can be in charge of the glitter and sprinkles!"

"Within reason," Mark added with a wink, stepping inside. He leaned in to kiss Emma's cheek, his lips cool from the winter air. "Good morning."

"Good morning," Emma replied, helping Olivia with her coat while trying not to get distracted by the way Mark was looking at her—like she was something precious and wonderful that he couldn't quite believe was real.

"Can we start now?" Olivia asked, already heading toward the kitchen. "I have so many ideas for our story cookies!"

They followed her into the kitchen, where she was already examining the array of supplies with wide-eyed wonder. "Look, Daddy! Miss Emma got angel cookie cutters and a tree and a heart!"

"I see that," Mark smiled, moving to stand beside Emma. "She thinks of everything, doesn't she?"

Emma felt her cheeks warm at the pride in his voice. "Well, we want these cookies to be special, right? Now, who's ready to get started?"

The next few hours passed in a whirl of flour, laughter, and Christmas music. Olivia proved to be an enthusiastic if somewhat messy helper, and Mark's attempts at precise cookie cutting were endearingly imperfect. Emma constantly paused just to take in moments—the way Olivia's tongue poked out in concentration as she carefully placed sprinkles, how Mark's hands looked covered in flour, the sound of their laughter mixing with the Christmas carols playing in the background.

"Okay," Olivia declared as they waited for the first batch to cool, "these angels are for me because I'm an angel in the play. And these trees are for when we decorated our tree together. And these hearts..."

She trailed off, looking between Emma and her father with wisdom beyond her years. "These hearts are because you love each other."

Emma felt Mark's hand find hers, their fingers intertwining naturally. "That's right, peanut," he said. "The hearts are very important to our story."

"I knew it," Olivia said proudly. "I told Gigi the other night after play practice that you two look at each other the same way her and Poppy do—all soft and happy."

Emma couldn't help but laugh, even as her heart swelled with emotion. "Out of the mouths of babes," she murmured, squeezing Mark's hand.

"Speaking of the play," Mark said, "should we practice your lines while these cool down?"

"Can we practice the whole nativity story?" Olivia asked excitedly. "Miss Emma can be Mary!"

What followed was perhaps the most unconventional nativity rehearsal ever performed in a kitchen, with flour-covered actors and cookie cutters standing in for props. Emma played Mary while Mark took on multiple roles, from Joseph to all three wise men, making Olivia giggle with his different voices.

As they acted out the sacred story, Emma was struck by how perfectly it fit their own journey—a story of faith, of following God's plan even when the path wasn't clear, of finding love and family in unexpected places.

"And lo, the angel of the Lord came upon them," Olivia recited perfectly, standing on a kitchen chair with her arms spread wide, "and the glory of the Lord shone round about them!"

"Beautiful, sweetheart," Mark praised, helping her down from the chair. "You're going to be amazing in the play."

"That's because I have the best teachers," Olivia declared, hugging first her father and then Emma. "Can we decorate the cookies now? They should be cool enough."

They gathered around the kitchen island, armed with frosting bags and decorating tools. Emma demonstrated some simple techniques she picked up on YouTube, showing them how to pipe outlines and fill them in, how to create patterns with different colors.

"Like this?" Mark asked, concentrating hard on a somewhat wobbly heart shape.

"Perfect," Emma assured him, even though it was anything but perfect in the technical sense. It was perfect because he'd made it, because of the love and effort he'd put into it.

"Miss Emma," Olivia said suddenly, pausing in her decorating, "are you going to spend Christmas with us?"

Emma glanced at Mark, unsure how to answer, but he was already smiling. "Actually," he said, "I was going to ask about that today. We'd love to have you join us for Christmas, Emma. You and your family."

"Really?" Emma felt tears prick at her eyes.

"Really," Mark confirmed.

"Please say yes," Olivia added, her eyes hopeful. "We can have breakfast together, and open presents, and maybe you could help me set up my new toys..."

"I'd love to," Emma managed, her voice thick with emotion. "We'd love to."

"Yay!" Olivia cheered, then immediately returned to her decorating with renewed enthusiasm. "We need to make extra special cookies for Christmas morning then!"

As they continued decorating, Emma was overwhelmed with gratitude. This was what healing looked like—flour-covered counters and imperfect hearts, Christmas carols and children's laughter, the warmth of belonging and the joy of new traditions being born.

"Hey," Mark said softly, catching her hand as she reached for more frosting. "You okay? You looked far away for a moment."

"I'm perfect," she assured him, leaning into his side. "Just... happy. Really, really happy."

He pressed a kiss to her temple, leaving a smudge of flour that made Olivia giggle. "Me too," he whispered. "Happier than I ever thought I could be again."

As the afternoon light began to fade, they surveyed their handiwork—dozens of cookies telling their story in sugar and frosting and love. Angels and trees, hearts and stars, each one imperfect but precious.

"These are the best cookies ever," Olivia declared proudly. "Santa is going to love them!"

"I think you're right," Emma agreed, watching as Mark carefully packed some cookies into containers to take home. "But maybe we should keep a few here for testing purposes?"

"Definitely," Mark agreed with a grin. "Quality control is very important."

They ended up on the couch, sharing cookies and hot chocolate while Olivia regaled them with more details about her role in the play. Emma found herself curled into Mark's side, his arm warm around her shoulders, while Olivia sat cross-legged on the floor, gesturing animatedly as she spoke.

This, Emma realized, was what she'd been missing all those years away from Laurel Ridge. Not just Mark, not just love, but this sense of completeness—of family and faith and the future, all wrapped up together in moments like these.

As if reading her thoughts, Mark squeezed her shoulders gently. "Thank you," he murmured.

"For what?"

"For coming home. For giving us a second chance. For making everything... better."

Emma turned her face up to his, not caring that Olivia was watching, and kissed him softly. "Thank you for waiting," she whispered against his lips. "For keeping a place for me in your heart all this time."

"Daddy," Olivia's voice broke in, "you're in loveeeeee!"

They broke apart laughing while Mark tried to look innocent. Outside, snow had begun to fall again, adding to the magical quality of the moment.

"We should probably head home before it gets worse," Mark said reluctantly, looking out at the gathering dusk.

As they gathered their things—cookies and coats and memories of a perfect afternoon—Emma felt that familiar surge of gratitude. For second chances and sugar cookies, for little girls who believed in angels, and for the kind of love that felt like coming home.

"Text me when you get home safe?" she asked as they stood at the door.

"Always," Mark promised, leaning in for one more kiss while Olivia made exaggerated gagging noises behind them.

"See you Monday, Miss Emma!" Olivia called as they headed to the truck. "Thank you for helping us make the best cookies ever!"

Emma stood in the doorway, watching until their taillights disappeared into the snowy evening. Inside, the kitchen still bore the happy evidence of their afternoon—flour dust and scattered sprinkles, the lingering scent of vanilla and sugar, and cookies in multiple containers.

She wouldn't clean up just yet, she decided. She wanted to savor this moment a little longer, this perfect snapshot of what love looked like when it came wrapped in flour dust and glitter, in children's laughter and gentle kisses.

Her phone buzzed with a text from Mark: "Home safe. Olivia's already planning what cookies we need to put on Santa's plate for Christmas morning. I love you."

Emma smiled, typing back: "I love you too. Both of you."

She moved through the house, turning on Christmas lights as evening settled in, and thought about how different everything felt from when she'd first returned to Laurel Ridge. Then, she'd been running from pain, seeking solace in familiar places. Now, she was running toward something—toward love and family, toward a future that felt brighter than any Christmas light.

In the kitchen, she picked up one of the heart-shaped cookies Mark had decorated. It was slightly lopsided, with uneven frosting and too many sprinkles on one side. But to Emma, it was perfect—just like their love story, with all its imperfect moments and unexpected turns leading to something beautiful and true.

She took a bite of the cookie and smiled, tasting love and promise and the sweet certainty of knowing she was exactly where she was meant to be.

Chapter 28

The week before Christmas brought a flurry of activity. Final play rehearsals at church, classroom parties at school, and the excited buzz of children counting down to winter break filled every moment. Emma was swept up in it all, her office becoming a parade of minor holiday-related injuries and emergency candy cane distributions.

Wednesday evening marked the last dress rehearsal for the Christmas play. Emma sat in the recreation hall, making last-minute adjustments to costumes, while Mark directed the children through their scenes. Olivia, in her complete angel costume, wings slightly askew, caught Emma's eye and gave a tiny wave between her lines.

"Looking good up there, angels," Mark called out. "Remember to stay in your positions until after Mary and Joseph reach the manger."

Emma watched him work with the children, marveling at his patience and gentle guidance. He caught her watching and smiled, that special smile that seemed reserved just for her, making her heart flutter.

"Miss Emma?" A small voice drew her attention. Courtney, one of the shepherd girls, stood beside her chair, holding her costume's sash. "Could you help me tie this? It keeps coming undone."

"Of course, sweetheart," Emma replied, kneeling to help. As she tied the sash, she noticed Courtney watching her with curious eyes.

"Are you going to marry Mr. Thompson?" the little girl asked suddenly, with the direct innocence only a child could manage.

Emma's hands stilled on the sash for a moment. "Why do you ask that?"

"Because you look at each other like my mommy and daddy do," Courtney said matter-of-factly. "And Olivia says you're part of their family now."

Before Emma could formulate a response, Mark's voice called out, "Places for the last scene, everyone!"

Courtney scampered off to join the other shepherds, leaving Emma with a warm flutter in her heart and thoughts she wasn't quite ready to examine too closely.

The rehearsal wrapped up successfully, with only minor costume malfunctions and forgotten lines to work out before tomorrow night's performance. As the children filed out with their parents, Olivia came running toward Emma and Mark.

"Did you see me?" she asked excitedly. "I remembered all my lines, and I didn't move until Mary and Joseph got to the manger!"

"You were perfect, sweetheart," Mark assured her, adjusting her crooked halo. "A real angel."

"The best angel in the whole play," Emma added, and was rewarded with one of Olivia's brilliant smiles.

"Can we get hot chocolate?" Olivia asked hopefully. "To celebrate the last rehearsal?"

Mark glanced at Emma, his eyes warm with invitation. "What do you say? Hot chocolate at the cafe?"

"I'd love to," Emma replied, already gathering her things.

They walked together outside toward Mark's truck, Olivia between them, chattering about tomorrow's performance and her excitement for Christmas break. It was already dark outside, but Christmas lights twinkled everywhere, making the town feel magical.

The cafe was warm and inviting, smelling of coffee and chocolate. They found a cozy corner table, and Mark went to order while Emma helped Olivia out of her coat.

"Miss Emma?" Olivia asked, her voice suddenly serious. "Are you really going to spend Christmas with us?"

"Of course," Emma assured her. "Your dad invited me and my family, remember?"

"Good," Olivia nodded solemnly. "Because I asked Santa for something special this year, and I need you to be there."

"Oh?" Emma's curiosity was piqued. "What did you ask for?"

But Olivia just smiled mysteriously. "It's a secret. But I think Santa's going to say yes, because Gigi says he knows what's in our hearts."

Mark returned with their drinks before Emma could probe further—hot chocolate with extra marshmallows for Olivia, peppermint mocha for Emma, and plain coffee for himself.

"What are you two conspiring about?" he asked, sliding into his seat beside Emma.

"Christmas secrets," Olivia replied importantly, carefully picking a marshmallow from her hot chocolate.

Mark raised an eyebrow at Emma, who shrugged slightly, still wondering about Olivia's mysterious Santa request. She felt Mark's hand find hers under the table, their fingers intertwining naturally, and she marveled at how such a simple touch could still send warmth spreading through her entire body.

They sat in the cozy coffee cafe, talking about tomorrow's performance and Christmas plans. Emma embraced it all, storing up these moments like precious gifts—the way Olivia's face was smudged with chocolate, how Mark's thumb traced absent patterns on her hand, the warmth of belonging that surrounded them all.

"Oh," Mark said suddenly, "I almost forgot. Mom wanted me to make sure you're coming to Christmas Eve dinner after church service"

Emma squeezed his hand. "I wouldn't miss it."

"With cookies and carols and everything!" Olivia added excitedly.

"That's right," Mark confirmed. "Mom's planning quite the feast."

As they finished their drinks and prepared to head home, all Emma could do was smile. Mark helped Olivia into her coat while Emma pulled on her gloves.

"Ready to go home, Liv?" Mark asked, taking Olivia's hand.

"Can Miss Emma come over?" Olivia asked hopefully. Just for a little while? We could show her the Christmas village we set up!"

Mark glanced at Emma. "What do you say? Want to see our slightly chaotic Christmas village?"

Emma pretended to consider it, though they all knew what her answer would be. "Well, how can I resist such an offer?"

The drive to Mark's house was quiet and peaceful, with Olivia humming Christmas carols in the back seat while the snow created a magical curtain around them.

Looking at Mark's profile in the glow of the dashboard lights, she realized that she could see it all so clearly now—not just Christmas together, but all the Christmases to come, all the everyday moments that would weave together to create a lifetime of love and family and faith.

Mark reached over and took her hand, bringing it to his lips for a soft kiss. "Penny for your thoughts?"

Emma smiled, squeezing his fingers. "Just thinking about how wonderful everything is. How blessed I feel to be here, with you both."

"Me too," he said. "More than you know."

When they pulled into his driveway, the house was already lit up with Christmas lights. Emma felt that familiar surge of belonging as they made their way inside, where the Christmas tree twinkled in the corner and the elaborate village display covered most of the coffee table.

"See?" Olivia said proudly, pulling Emma toward the village. "Daddy and I set it up last night. We put the skating rink in the middle, just like at the festival!"

Emma knelt beside the coffee table, admiring the detailed miniature scene. There was indeed a tiny skating rink, complete with miniature skaters, surrounded by little shops and houses dusted with artificial snow. A small church stood on a hill overlooking the village, its windows glowing warmly.

"It's beautiful," she said sincerely. "You did a wonderful job."

"It's like our town," Olivia explained, pointing out different features. "See? This could be the school, and here's the coffee cafe, and this house could be yours..."

Emma felt Mark's hand on her shoulder as he knelt beside them. "It does look a lot like Laurel Ridge, doesn't it?" he agreed. "All it's missing is an angel for the church."

"Oh!" Olivia's eyes lit up. "Can we put my angel ornament there? The one Gigi gave me?"

"Good idea, peanut. Why don't you go get it off the little Christmas tree in your bedroom?"

As Olivia darted away, Mark pulled Emma to her feet and into his arms. "Thank you," he said softly.

"For what?"

"For being you. For being here. For making this Christmas so special. For loving us both so completely. For coming home."

Emma wrapped her arms around his neck, standing on tiptoe to kiss him gently. "Thank you for being my home to come back to."

The sound of Olivia's returning footsteps broke them apart. They watched as she carefully placed her angel ornament atop the church, completing their perfect miniature world.

"Now it's just right," Olivia declared. She yawned, the long day catching up with her.

"Time for bed, I think," Mark said, checking his watch. "You need to rest up for your big performance tomorrow."

"Will you come say goodnight, Miss Emma?" Olivia asked hopefully.

"Of course."

After helping Olivia change into her pajamas and watching as Mark tucked her in, Emma sat on the edge of the bed while Olivia said her prayers. Her heart melted as the little girl added a special thank you, "for bringing Miss Emma home to us."

"Goodnight, sweetheart," Emma whispered, kissing Olivia's forehead. "Sleep tight."

"Goodnight, Miss Emma. I love you."

The words, spoken so simply and naturally, brought tears to Emma's eyes. "I love you too, sweet girl."

Back downstairs, Mark pulled Emma close again, both of them gazing at the Christmas village with its new angel guardian. "She really does love you, you know," he said softly. "We both do."

"I love you both so much," Emma replied, her voice thick with emotion. "Sometimes I can't believe how perfectly God brought us all together."

"His timing is always perfect." Mark agreed, pressing a kiss to her temple.

Emma gathered her things and stepped outside just as Andrew's truck pulled into the driveway. She waved to Mark, who stood in the doorway, his expression warm and soft, and her heart swelled once again. As soon as she slid into the passenger seat, silence filled the truck. Andrew had that look, the one that told her a flood of questions was waiting to spill.

Emma smiled to herself, feeling more ready than ever to share every detail.

"So," Andrew finally broke the silence, his tone teasing as he put the truck in drive and backed down the driveway. "The Christmas village, huh?"

Emma chuckled, glancing out the window as the snow slowed to a gentle flurry. "Yes, it's adorable. Olivia was so proud of it. And I think she might be plotting something with Santa."

"Plotting?" Andrew arched an eyebrow. "That child is a mastermind, that one. You may need to keep an eye on your stockings come Christmas Eve.

Emma smiled, remembering how wide-eyed Olivia had been as she talked about her Christmas wish. "Whatever it is, I know it's coming from a place of love."

"I'm happy for you, Em," Andrew said, his voice sincere now. "Really, I am. Mark and Olivia, the entire Thompson family are good people, and... well, I... I really couldn't be happier for you or them."

Emma turned to look at him, her heart swelling with gratitude for her brother, who had been her rock through so many hard times. "Thank you. For always supporting me, no matter where I was in my life."

Andrew gave her a sidelong look that was both affectionate and exasperated. "I knew you'd figure things out. You just needed to do it at your own pace."

Chapter 29

The night of the Christmas play arrived with perfect winter weather—just enough snow to make everything feel magical, but not enough to keep anyone away. Emma stood behind a curtain that had been hung behind the stage in the recreation hall, helping with last-minute costume adjustments, while excited children buzzed around her.

"Miss Emma!" Olivia's voice caught her attention. "Can you fix my halo? It keeps sliding down."

Emma knelt down, carefully adjusting the wire halo that had indeed slipped askew. "There you go, sweet girl. Perfect."

"Are you nervous?" Olivia asked, fidgeting with her angel wings.

"A little," Emma admitted with a smile. "But you know what? It's okay to be nervous. It means you care about doing your best."

"Daddy says that too," Olivia nodded solemnly. "He says the butterflies in our tummy are really just excitement wearing a costume."

Emma laughed softly, touched by Mark's way with words. "Your daddy is very wise."

She could hear his voice from the other side of the curtain, greeting parents as they arrived. The recreation hall was filling up quickly. It seemed like the whole town had turned out for the annual Christmas play.

"Come on, kids, it's showtime! Gather round a second and let's say a quick prayer," Martha called out.

Emma gave Olivia one last hug. "Break a leg, sweetheart. You're going to be amazing."

As she walked around the curtain, she caught Mark's eye. His smile when he saw her was bright enough to light up the entire hall.

"Everything okay back there?" he asked as she approached.

"Perfect," she assured him. "All angels' halos are secure and accounted for."

He caught her hand briefly, squeezing it before letting go.

The lights dimmed, and Mark moved to center stage to welcome everyone. Emma watched him with pride as he spoke about the meaning of Christmas and the hard work all the children had put into the performance.

The play began, and Emma watched as each scene unfolded. Mary and Joseph made their way to Bethlehem. The innkeeper turned them away (though he did seem a bit more apologetic than strictly necessary), and then it was time for the angels to appear.

Olivia's entrance was perfect. She remembered all her lines, her halo stayed in place, and her voice rang out clear and strong: "Fear not: for, behold, I bring you good tidings of great joy, which shall be to all people."

Emma felt tears prick at her eyes, overwhelmed by the beauty of the moment and the pure faith shining in Olivia's face as she delivered her lines. When she glanced at Mark, she saw the same emotion reflected in his eyes.

The rest of the play went smoothly, with only minor mishaps—a shepherd briefly forgot his lines but was prompted by a loud whisper from behind the curtain, and one of the wise men almost dropped his gift but recovered admirably. Throughout it all, Olivia stood proudly with the other angels, beaming with joy.

As the final carol began—'Silent Night' sung by all the children—Emma felt Mark slide into the seat beside her. His hand found hers in the darkness, and she leaned into him slightly, both of them watching Olivia sing her heart out.

When the play ended, the applause was thunderous. Parents rushed forward with cameras and flowers, and the hall filled with excited chatter and congratulations. Olivia came running off the stage and threw herself into their arms.

"Did you see? Did you see me remember all my lines?"

"You were perfect, peanut," Mark assured her, lifting her up for a proper hug. "The best angel in the whole show."

"Really?" Olivia turned to Emma for confirmation.

"Really," Emma agreed, smoothing a stray curl that had escaped from under the halo. "You made us so proud."

"Indeed, she did," a familiar voice added, and they turned to find Clair approaching, followed by Eli and several other family members. "Our little angel was magnificent."

What followed was a whirlwind of hugs and congratulations, photos and proud grandparent moments. Through it all, Emma found herself included naturally in the family circle, with Clair's arm around her shoulders and Andrew snapping pictures of all of them together.

"Ice cream to celebrate?" Mark suggested once the crowd had begun to thin out. "I know a certain angel who deserves a treat."

"Can Miss Emma come too?" Olivia asked, still bubbling with post-performance excitement.

"Of course," Mark smiled, his hand finding Emma's again. "Miss Emma is family."

They ended up at the ice cream parlor, which had stayed open late specifically for the after-play crowd. Olivia, still in her angel costume (minus the wings, which were safely in the car), proudly ordered a sundae with extra sprinkles while Mark and Emma shared a banana split.

"Did you see everyone crying during 'Silent Night'?" Olivia asked between bites. "Even Martha was wiping her eyes!"

"That's because it was beautiful," Emma told her. "You all did such a wonderful job."

"And now it's really almost Christmas," Olivia continued excitedly. "Just a few more days! Are you excited about the Christmas Eve service, Miss Emma? Gigi says it's going to be extra special this year."

Emma caught the look that passed between Mark and Clair at Olivia's words, but before she could question it, Andrew joined them at the table, pulling up a chair.

"Room for one more? I heard there was celebratory ice cream social happening."

The conversation shifted to Christmas plans and memories of past plays, but Emma couldn't shake the feeling that something was brewing—something wonderful and mysterious that everyone but her seemed to know about.

Later that night, after they'd said goodbye to everyone and Olivia was whisked off with Eli and Clair for a special great-grandparent's sleepover, Mark walked Emma to her door.

"Stay for a while?" she asked. "I'll make coffee."

Inside, they settled on the couch with steaming mugs, the Christmas tree lights casting a warm light over everything. Emma curled into Mark's side, savoring the warmth and closeness.

"Thank you," she said.

"For what?"

"For everything. For letting me be a part of your life, part of Olivia's life. For giving us this second chance."

Mark set his coffee down and turned to face her fully. "Emma," he said, his hand coming up to cup her cheek, "you don't have to thank me for that. Having you in our lives... it's the best gift I could have ever asked for."

He kissed her then, soft and sweet, and Emma felt her heart overflow with love for this man who had waited for her, who had kept a place for her in his heart all these years.

When they parted, Mark rested his forehead against hers. "I should go," he said reluctantly. "Early day tomorrow."

"I know," Emma sighed, but neither of them moved for a moment, both wanting to hold on to the perfect peace of this moment.

Finally, Mark stood, pulling Emma to her feet with him. At the door, he kissed her once more, then smiled that special smile that made her knees weak.

"Sweet dreams, my love," he whispered. "I'll see you tomorrow."

Emma watched from the doorway until his taillights disappeared down the driveway, then went back inside to get ready for bed. As she was changing into her pajamas, her phone buzzed with a text from Olivia:

"Goodnight Miss Emma! Thank you for helping me be the best angel! I love you!"

Followed by one from Mark:

"Olivia insisted on sending you a goodnight text. I second her sentiments, minus the angel part. Though you are pretty heavenly. I love you."

Chapter 30

Christmas Eve dawned bright and clear, with fresh snow blanketing Laurel Ridge in pristine white. Emma stood at her window, watching the early morning sun turn everything to sparkling diamond dust, her heart full of anticipation for the day ahead.

Her phone buzzed with a text from Mark: *"Merry Christmas Eve, beautiful. Can't wait to see you at church tonight."*

Emma smiled, typing back: *"Merry Christmas Eve to you both."*

The day stretched before her, filled with last-minute Christmas preparations and the sweet anticipation of evening church service. She had already wrapped all her gifts—including special ones for Mark and Olivia that she'd spent days choosing carefully—and dropped them off at Clair's house for tomorrow's celebration.

Emma spent the afternoon reading and then getting ready for the evening service. She selected a deep red sweater dress, paired with the cream-colored scarf. As she was fixing her hair, her phone buzzed with another text, this time from Olivia:

"Miss Emma! Can you come over now? Daddy's not very good at doing hair and I want to look pretty for church!"

Laughing, Emma grabbed her coat and headed out. The drive to Mark's house was beautiful, with Christmas lights beginning to twinkle as the winter afternoon faded into evening. She found Olivia waiting at the door, already wearing her Christmas dress but with her hair in tangles.

"Thank goodness you're here," Mark said, looking adorably overwhelmed. "I tried to do her hair the way she asked, but…"

"But Daddy made it worse," Olivia finished matter-of-factly, making them both laugh.

Emma spent the next half hour carefully brushing and styling Olivia's hair into perfect curls. When she finished, Olivia twirled in front of the mirror, beaming with delight.

"Perfect!" she declared. "Now I look like a proper Christmas angel!"

"Yes, you do," Mark agreed, coming to stand beside Emma. He slipped an arm around her waist and pressed a kiss to her temple. "Thank you for saving us from a hair disaster."

They arrived at the church early, as Mark needed to help set up for the service. The historic church building was already filling with familiar faces—friends and neighbors all gathered to celebrate the holy night. Emma helped Olivia find Clair in their usual pew while Mark disappeared to handle his duties.

The church looked beautiful, decorated with evergreen boughs and white candles. The massive Christmas tree near the altar sparkled with white lights, and poinsettias lined the aisles. Emma sat beside Olivia, who was practically vibrating with excitement.

"Miss Emma," Olivia whispered, tugging on her sleeve, "do you remember what I told Santa I wanted for Christmas?"

"The special secret?" Emma whispered back. "No, you never told me what it was."

Olivia's eyes twinkled mysteriously. "You'll find out soon," she promised, then fell silent as the small organ began to play.

The service was beautiful, filled with familiar carols and the timeless story of Christ's birth. When it came time to light the candles for "Silent Night," Emma was overwhelmed with emotion as the flame was passed from person to person, filling the church with golden light.

Mark had joined them by then, standing close beside her as they held their candles and sang. In the flickering light, Emma could see tears in his eyes that matched her own—tears of joy, of gratitude, of love so deep it could only be expressed in quiet wonder.

After the final blessing, people began to file out into the snowy night.

"Ready to head to Grandma's?" Mark asked, helping Olivia into her coat.

"Actually," he continued as he turned toward Emma, suddenly looking nervous, "could we stay here for just a moment? There's something I'd like to do first."

Emma nodded, curious about his tone. She watched as he whispered something to his mother, who at once gathered Olivia with a knowing smile and headed for the door with the rest of the family.

"Mark?" Emma questioned as he took her hand and led her toward the altar. "What's going on?"

The church was almost empty now, lit only by the Christmas tree and the candles that still burned softly. Mark turned to face her, taking both her hands in his. Emma's heart began to race as she realized what might be happening.

"Emma," he began softly, his voice full of emotion, "when you came back to Laurel Ridge, I thought God was giving us a chance to heal old wounds, to find closure for what we lost years ago. But He had so much more in store for us. He was giving us a chance to build something new and beautiful—not just for us, but for Olivia, too."

Emma felt tears begin to fall as Mark continued, his own eyes shining.

"You've brought so much joy into our lives—into my life. Your love for Olivia, your faith in me, your gentle spirit that makes everything better just by being near... I can't imagine my life without you in it anymore. I don't want to."

He reached into his pocket and pulled out a small box, then dropped to one knee before her. Emma's hand flew to her mouth as he opened the box to reveal a beautiful ring—delicate and vintage-looking, with a single diamond surrounded by smaller stones that caught the candlelight and sparkled like stars.

"Emma Whitman," Mark's voice was thick with emotion, "will you marry me? Will you be my wife, Olivia's mother, and my partner in whatever adventure God has planned for us?"

For a moment, Emma couldn't speak past the joyful tears that streamed down her face. Then, with all the love in her heart, she whispered, "Yes. Yes, to everything. Always yes."

Mark's hands shook slightly as he slipped the ring onto her finger, then stood and pulled her into his arms. Their kiss was soft and sweet, filled with promises and dreams and thanksgiving.

A small squeal from the doorway broke them apart, and they turned to see Olivia running toward them, unable to contain herself any longer. She threw herself into their embrace, and they caught her together, forming a perfect family circle.

"She said yes?" Olivia asked excitedly, though she clearly already knew the answer.

"She said yes," Mark confirmed, his voice full of joy.

"That was my Christmas wish!" Olivia declared proudly. "I asked Santa to make you my mom!"

Emma felt fresh tears spring to her eyes as she hugged Olivia close. "Oh, sweetheart!"

The rest of the family began returning to the room—Clair, eyes shining with happy tears; Eli, his face radiating pride; Andrew and Harper, and even her parents, both crying and smiling. They were all together, united in the moment.

As congratulations and hugs were shared all around, Emma looked at her ring sparkling in the Christmas tree lights. It was perfect—elegant but not flashy, timeless, but unique. Just like their love story.

"Do you like it?" Mark asked softly, coming up behind her and wrapping his arms around her waist.

"I love it," she whispered, leaning back against him. "It's perfect. Everything is perfect."

They made their way to Eli and Clair's house for the traditional Christmas Eve gathering, where more congratulations and celebrations awaited. The house was warm and festive, filled with the scents of the holiday season, and the sound of carols playing softly in the background.

As Emma sat on the couch later that evening, with Olivia curled up beside her and Mark's arm around them both, she marveled at how perfectly God had brought everything together.

"Penny for your thoughts?" Mark murmured in her ear.

Emma smiled, touching her ring. "Just thinking about how blessed I am. How perfect God's timing is."

"Speaking of timing," Mark said with a grin, "Olivia has another request."

"Oh?"

"She wants to know if we can get married at Christmas next year. She thinks it would be romantic."

Emma laughed softly, looking down at Olivia, sleeping like an angel. "You know what? I think she might be right about that."

Chapter 31

Christmas morning dawned with the kind of magical perfection that seemed almost too good to be true. Emma woke early, watching the sun rise over the fresh snow while admiring her engagement ring in the pale morning light. Her phone buzzed with a text from Mark:

"Merry Christmas, my love. Olivia's already up and asking when you'll be here. She said Santa brought something special just for you."

Emma smiled, typing back: *"Merry Christmas! Tell her Andrew and I will be there soon. I love you both."*

She got ready quickly, choosing a soft green sweater and her most festive Christmas earrings. The drive to Mark's house was beautiful, with the morning sun making the snow sparkle like diamonds. Mark and Olivia stepped out on the porch, Olivia still in her Christmas pajamas, as she parked her SUV.

"Miss Emma!" Olivia called out, running to meet her. "Merry Christmas! Santa came, and he left something special just for you!"

"Did he now?" Emma laughed, accepting Olivia's enthusiastic hug while Mark approached more sedately, though his smile was just as bright.

"Merry Christmas," he murmured, pulling her close for a kiss that made her toes curl despite the cold.

Inside, the house was warm and festive, with Christmas music playing softly and the tree lights twinkling. The smell of coffee and cinnamon rolls filled the air.

"Breakfast first," Mark declared as Olivia bounced impatiently near the presents. "Then we can see what Santa brought."

They gathered around the kitchen table, where Mark had prepared a feast of cinnamon rolls, bacon, and fresh fruit. Emma's heart swelled as she watched him serve Olivia, thinking about all the Christmas mornings to come when they would do this together as a family.

"Okay, now can we open presents?" Olivia asked the moment the last bite was finished.

"Yes, now we can open presents," Mark laughed, leading them to the living room.

Olivia immediately dove for a specially wrapped package, bringing it to Emma with barely contained excitement. "This one's for you! It's from Santa!"

Emma accepted the gift, curious about what could have both Olivia and Mark looking so pleased with themselves. She carefully unwrapped it to reveal a beautiful leather-bound photo album. Opening it, she gasped.

The first page held a photo of her and Mark from their high school days, followed by recent pictures of them at the Winter Festival, decorating cookies, and at the Christmas play. But it was the following pages that brought tears to her eyes—they were blank, with spaces labeled "Our Wedding," "Our First Christmas as a Family," and "Our Future Adventures."

"Do you like it?" Olivia asked anxiously. "Daddy helped me make it, but it was my idea!"

"Oh, sweetheart," Emma pulled her close for a hug, "I love it. It's perfect."

The rest of the morning passed in a blur of wrapping paper and joy. Olivia was thrilled with her gifts, especially the art supplies Emma had chosen for her.

As Olivia played with her new toys, Mark pulled Emma onto the couch beside him. "I have one more gift for you," he said, pulling a small package from behind a cushion.

Inside, Emma found a delicate silver ornament in the shape of an angel. Engraved on its wings were the words "Our First Christmas—2024" and on the back, "The Beginning of Forever."

"It's beautiful," she whispered, touching it gently.

"I thought we could start our own collection," Mark explained. "One for every Christmas together."

Emma kissed him softly, pouring all her love into the gesture. "It's perfect. Just like everything else about this Christmas."

They spent the rest of the morning in peaceful contentment, watching Olivia play while sharing quiet moments together. Around noon, they started getting ready to head to Mark's grandparents' house, where the warmth and joy of Christmas would be shared by both of their families. It wasn't just a gathering; it was the start of a future where everyone they loved could be together, celebrating the holiday.

"Miss Emma," Olivia called from her room where she was changing, "can you help me with my Christmas dress?"

Emma found her struggling with buttons and smoothed the festive red velvet into place. As she helped Olivia with her hair, the little girl asked, "When you marry Daddy, can I call you Mom?"

Emma's hands stilled for a moment, her heart overflowing with emotion. "Sweetheart, you can call me whatever makes you comfortable. I love you no matter what."

Olivia was quiet for a moment, thinking. "I think... I think I'd like to call you Mom. Because that's what you are in my heart already."

Emma hugged her tightly, trying not to cry and ruin her makeup. "I'd be honored to be your mom, sweet girl. So very honored."

They arrived at Clair's to find the house already full of people from both sides of their families and the delicious smells of Christmas dinner.

The afternoon was filled with food, laughter, and the joyful hum of Christmas celebrations. Emma's fingers instinctively brushed over her engagement ring, still marveling at how perfectly everything had fallen into place. From her spot by the tree, she watched Mark kneel on the floor with Olivia, helping her show off her new toys to her eager cousins. In the kitchen, Clair moved about with the confidence of someone in her element, offering everyone an endless array of cookies, while Eli stood by the fireplace, deep in conversation with Andrew. Across the room, Emma's mother flitted about with her camera, capturing every smiling face, while her dad sat nearby, his eyes brimming with pride and happiness. Harper sat beside their father, her eyes sparkling as she caught Emma's gaze. With a soft smile, she mouthed, "I love you."

Later, as the sun began to set and the Christmas lights twinkled more brightly against the darkening sky, Emma stood by the window watching the snow fall. Mark came up behind her, wrapping his arms around her waist.

"Happy?" he asked softly.

"More than I ever thought possible," she replied, leaning back against him. "This has been an amazing Christmas."

"Thank you for saying yes," he murmured, pressing a kiss to her temple. "To everything—to coming home, to giving us a second chance, to becoming my wife and Olivia's mother."

"Mom!" Olivia's voice called from across the room. "Gigi says it's time for Christmas carols!"

Emma was momentarily taken aback by the new title, but her heart swelled with warmth as Mark gently squeezed her hand, as if wordlessly acknowledging the significance of the moment. They moved to join their families around the piano, where Clair had already begun playing the gentle, familiar strains of "Silent Night."

As they sang together, Emma looked around the room. Each of their families together and happy. This was what home felt like. This was what love looked like when God's perfect plan came together.

Later that evening, Mark pulled her close and asked, "What are you thinking about?"

"About how different everything is from last Christmas," Emma replied. "About how lost I was. About how terrified yet confidant I felt about leaving Pittsburgh, and how perfectly God knew what I needed—what we all needed."

"He knew," Mark agreed, touching her ring. "He knew exactly when to bring you back to us."

"To bring us all together," Emma corrected, thinking of Olivia calling her 'Mom' for the first time.

Mark kissed her then, soft and sweet and full of promise. When they parted, he rested his forehead against hers. "Merry Christmas, future Mrs. Thompson."

"Merry Christmas, Mr. Thompson," Emma whispered back.

Outside, the snow continued to fall softly, adding to the magical quality of the night. But inside, wrapped in the warmth of love and family and faith, Emma knew she had received the greatest gift of all—a second chance at love that had become something more beautiful than she could have ever imagined.

Leave A Review

If you enjoyed this book, please consider leaving an honest review on Amazon or Goodreads.

Visit Our Website:

www.tarabaisden.com

Visit Our Amazon Author Page HERE

Find Us On Social Media:

Facebook

Instagram

TikTok

Pinterest

GoodReads